The Wedding Planner's Daughter
Playing Cupid

Coleen Murtagh Paratore is the author of several books that have been published in the US. She lives in Albany, New York, with her husband and three sons. She is a hopeless romantic and lifelong believer in the magic of Cape Cod.

The first book about Willa Havisham, *The Wedding Planner's Daughter*, is already available in the UK and the third title, *Star-Crossed Summer*, is coming soon.

The Wedding Planner's
Daughter

Playing Cupid

Coleen Murtagh Paratore

MACMILLAN CHILDREN'S BOOKS

First published in the USA 2006 by Simon & Schuster Books for Young Readers
First published in the UK 2007 by Macmillan Children's Books

This edition published 2008 by Macmillan Children's Books
a division of Macmillan Publishers Limited
20 New Wharf Road, London N1 9RR
Basingstoke and Oxford
www.panmacmillan.com

Associated companies throughout the world

ISBN 978-0-330-44298-5

1 3 5 7 9 8 6 4 2

A CIP catalogue record for this book is available from the British Library.

Printed and bound in Great Britain by Mackays of Chatham plc, Kent

To my mother,
Peg Spain Murtagh,
the queen of hearts,
who took me on the bus to the library
and shared her great love of books.
— C. M. P.

Contents

Juniors Don't Date Freshmen

This wimpled, whining, purblind, wayward boy;
This senior-junior, giant-dwarf . . . Cupid;

— William Shakespeare, *Love's Labour's Lost*

'But what about Cupid?' I ask my friend Tina. Ever since Tina's Aunt Amber started a matchmaking company called The Perfect Ten, Tina thinks the way to true love is finding the boy you have ten important things in common with.

'*Cupid?*' Tina stops writing and laughs. 'You are such a dreamer, Willa. What's that flying baby with a bow and arrow got to do with love?'

'Cupid's got everything to do with love. Cupid's the magic and the mystery, the goosebumps and heart-thumps, the lightning bolt you can't explain, but . . .'

'Oh, Willa, get your head out of that Shakespeare book. The numbers don't lie. Tanner and I are compatibly perfect for each other.'

Tina's Bambi eyes roll from east to west, and set on Tanner McGee. He's sitting at the varsity soccer table. Tall and strong with a lifeguard tan, Tanner's so gorgeous he glows. Girls in the dining hall drool dreamily as Tanner stuffs an entire slice of pizza into his mouth. Tina smiles and takes a princess-size nibble of hers.

'See!' Tina flips her blonde hair back and writes in her notebook again. 'Favourite food? *Pizza*. Tanner likes pizza. I like pizza. Favourite sport? *Soccer*. Tanner likes soccer. I like soccer.'

'Are those the ten questions?' I ask. 'You've got to be kidding . . .'

'No, Willa. I'm making up my own questions. Aunt Amber's got a patent on hers. But food and sports are important, right?' Tina flips her hair back again. 'And we have lots of other things in common, too. Tanner has brown eyes. I have brown eyes. Tanner's name starts with "T." My name starts with—'

'Tina, stop.'

I love Tina Belle. She's my best friend. But sometimes I've just got to whack her back to reality. 'You've just described half of Bramble Academy. Everybody likes pizza. Everybody likes soccer. You haven't even met this boy. And besides, Tanner's a junior. You're a freshman. Juniors don't date freshmen.'

'Really, Willa?' Now Tina's getting mad. 'Well, maybe juniors don't date freshmen in those drippy-do Nancy Drew books you read. But in real life they do.'

'Actually, Tina, I prefer Dickens. And Shakespeare, of course. Wasn't Dr Swaminathan so dramatic reading *Hamlet* this morning? It's like we were in the Globe Theatre in London. "*To be, or not to be: that is the question . . .*"'

'Well, I think Shakespeare's a sleeper, but Dr Swammy could be on the soaps. Speaking of which . . . there's Mackie and Mona. *One –*' Tina sticks her thumb in the air – 'he's a junior; she's a freshman. And Booker and Babs. *Two . . .*'

'Tina, those are actors on TV. This is Bramble, Cape Cod, Massachusetts. Around here, juniors don't date freshmen. Besides, Tanner's gorgeous and . . .'

'Thanks a lot, Willa.'

'Oh, Tina, you know you're beautiful.'

Without a doubt Tina is the prettiest girl in the freshman class. Ruby Snivler's second. I guess *maybe* I'm in the top ten, which isn't bragging since there are only twelve girls in the whole class.

Tina's not done. 'And since when are you the dating expert, Willa? I know you matched up your mother and Sam, but other than one date with . . .'

'Hey, Willa. How's it going?'

I turn around and there he is. My one date. Joseph Francis Kennelly. *JFK.* Conjured up before me. In the flesh. Sea-blue eyes. Sandy hair. That dimple to die for. He's even gotten cuter if that's possible.

Boing. Cupid's arrow hits. My heart's beating like a bongo and my hands are shaking so bad that the brass buttons on the cuff of my uniform blazer are clanking like cymbals on my soda can, *clank, clank, clank.*

Breathe, Willa, breathe.

'Hi, Joseph . . . when did you get back?'

Shortly after our one and only date, JFK's family moved to Minnesota. Then last month we heard Mr Kennelly might be named publisher of the *Cape Cod Times*. Tina burst in during Sunday brunch at the Bramblebriar Inn, where I live. 'JFK's coming back! JFK's coming back!' Our guests looked up in alarm.

'Not that JFK,' my mother assured them. 'More coffee anyone?'

'We got in yesterday,' Joseph says. 'I'm still unpacking my stuff.'

'Well, welcome home,' I say. 'I missed you.' *Oh no*. 'I mean, we all missed you.' *Oh no, that's even worse.*

There's a mountain-sized moment of silence.

'So what are you doing for Halloween, Joe?' Tina throws me a life preserver. 'Want to go candy-collecting? A bunch of us are going. You don't need a costume.'

'Yeh, OK.' JFK looks at me. 'Sounds good.' He's still looking at me.

Jump in, Willa. Jump in.

'And then later on,' I say, 'we're having a party

at the Inn, in the barn.' I am making this up on the spot. 'Lots of food, music . . .'

'Sounds good.' JFK's face is red. He drops a book. 'See ya.'

'Way to go, Willa.' Tina is shocked. 'A party, huh? What will Stella say?'

Good question. My mother isn't the easiest person to deal with. After my first father died in a tragic accident before I was even born, Stella opened a wedding-planning business to support us, but her own heart was too broken to ever love again. And she wrote a rule book the size of a dictionary to make sure I kept my mind on school. I spent years wishing for a father, trying to find 'Mr Right' – the right husband for Stella, the right father for me – with no luck. Then Nana somehow convinced Stella to come home to Cape Cod and then Sam Gracemore moved in next door and he turned out to be my English teacher, and the rest, as they say, is history. Except for the rule book. Stella still loves those rules.

'I don't know, Tina. I hope she says, 'Great idea, have fun,' but I have a feeling it will be much more complicated than that.'

'Tell Stella and Sam to think of it as a . . . *community service*,' Tina says.

'What?' I cough on my cheeseburger.

At Freshman Meeting this morning, I was elected Community Service Leader. Actually 'elected' is stretching the taffy. No one else volunteered. But I kept hearing Nana saying, 'We're lucky ducks, Willa. We've got our health, home and a happy family, and when you've got a lot, you've got to give a lot back,' and finally my hand went up.

'Tina, how is a party in the barn considered *community service*?'

Tina huffs like I'm hopeless. 'Think of it as a way to bring the guys and girls in our class together, to see who's compatible, who can dance . . .'

'Tina, that's not a community service. That's a *dating* service.'

Tina crinkles her eyebrows and smiles. 'Exactly, Willa. What's the problem? Are you forgetting who's back in Bramble?'

JFK's back. JFK's back. The bell rings.

'OK, Tina. I'll give it a try. Come on, we're late for class.'

'Ooh, fun,' Tina says. 'A party in the barn. Now, what are we going to wear?'

2

Be a Leaper

Yet mark'd I where the bolt of Cupid fell:
It fell upon a little western flower . . .
— Shakespeare, *A Midsummer Night's Dream*

My mouth full of liquorice, my heart full of
hope, I nearly skip home along Main Street. *JFK's*
back. JFK's back. The yard by Bramble United
Community, 'BUC,' is filled with giant sunflowers,
bobbing like they're talking in the breeze. A black
face rises up from the yellow sea. Mum waves and
walks toward me with a bouquet.

'Hey little sister.' Mum gives me a hug. 'How's
high school?'

'So far so good, Mum.'

Mum is actually Sulamina Mum, the minister
of BUC, 'a home for every heart'. In some ways it's

odd that I call her Mum, when I almost always call my own mother Stella, but somehow the name just suits Sulamina – she just is . . . Mum. Every weekend, people from all different religions 'come together to be grateful,' as Mum says. Just about everyone in Bramble belongs. BUC is never boring and the bagels are good.

'Who you playing Cupid for these days?' Mum says. Mum knows I hitched up Stella and Sam and she gives me credit for Nana and Gramp Tweed too. My grandmother owned the candy store in town and Mr Tweed owned the bookstore. I invited them to a picnic. They did all the rest. After their wedding, which I helped plan, they combined their businesses into Sweet Bramble Books, happy as taffy on teeth. It's great for me too. Now I can buy my two favourite things, books and candy, one-stop shopping.

'Got a dark handsome stranger up your sleeve for me?' Mum asks all serious. She lets that sink in a bit, and then starts in with her deep-belly laugh.

'My matchmaking days are done, Mum. Right now I need to find a cause.'

'A cause?'

'You know . . . a worthy cause, a charitable need, raise some money, do something good. I'm the new Community Service Leader for our class and I'm supposed to, quote . . . unquote, "Scout out an opportunity to make a better Bramble and then organize and inspire classmates to participate." Got any ideas?'

'Well, there's lots of ways to make a difference, Willa. I'd say pick a cause you care about. Something close to your heart. Then you'll surely succeed.'

I tell Mum that JFK is back and how I invited him for Halloween and how now all I have to do is convince Stella to let me have a party in the barn . . .

Mum bursts out laughing. 'Well aren't you something, little sister. When I was young it was the fella who did the asking out.' A sad look flits across Mum's face. 'Here, give these to Stella.' Mum hands me the sunflowers. 'Maybe they'll help.'

'Did you have a fella, Mum?'

'Oh, no . . .'

'Come on, Mum. Tell me.'

Mum squints at me. 'Nothing 'bout love gets past you, does it honey?'

She sits on the step. I sit down too. We cast very different-sized shadows.

'You wouldn't know it looking at me now, but when I was a high-school senior I had a mighty fine man calling on me. *Mmmm, mmmm, mmmm.* When Riley Truth looked at me, my knees'd turn to pudding. Chocolate pudding.'

'What happened to him, Mum?' This is exciting.

'Well, right around the time I got my calling for the seminary, Riley got his calling too. From the United States Army. He went overseas and I went north and north and north. Then the years piled up and letters stopped coming . . .' Mum's lips quiver. She wipes her eyes. ''Nough about that.'

'Well, where is Riley now? Why don't you call him, Mum?'

'Oh no, honey. What's over's over.'

'But look at how mushy you still are, Mum. That's Cupid working. And I bet Riley Truth still loves you too. You should track him down.'

'Oh, no, Willa. I couldn't.'

'Yes you could, Mum. If I was brave enough to invite JFK . . .'

'Stop it, Willa. Now.' Mum's voice is angry. She foists herself up.

It's like I've been slapped. I've never seen Mum mad.

She turns to me. 'I'm sorry, Willa.' Her kind brown eyes are glistening. 'It's just I'm a big old chicken hawk, *squawk, squawk . . .*'

'It's OK, Mum. Don't be afraid. Be a leaper.'

'A what?'

'A leaper. Come on, Mum. You're the minister. Take a leap of faith. Believe in yourself. Just leap right over the scary part and land on the other side.'

Mum sticks her chin up, sways her head side to side. 'A leaper.' She laughs. 'I like that. I might use it in my sermon Sunday. But I'm not promising any—'

'Gotta go, Mum. I'm late.'

The sunflowers are garden-warm in my arms, but when I see the Bramble Library, I turn cold. There's a strange sign on the door. 'Closed Until Further Notice.' The shutters are drawn on the windows. I hope Mrs Saperstone is OK. Sam will know. I hurry home.

The Bramblebriar Inn is dressed for autumn: pots of red and yellow chrysanthemums, pumpkins, cornstalks, goofy scarecrows, maple leaves dancing on the cobblestone fence. Guests are relaxing in wicker chairs, reading, talking, napping. There's a short plump man in a fancy suit and a tall plump lady in a mink coat reading the Bramble Board. New rich guests I bet. Sam started the tradition of the Bramble Board. Now I put up the quotes. Today it reads:

It is by spending oneself that one becomes rich.
– Sarah Bernhardt

'Mom, Sam, I'm home!'

My parents are in the kitchen. It's our busiest time of day. Sam is lifting a pie out of the oven. Stella's arranging miniature quiches on a tray. Butternut squash soup is simmering on the stove. *Hmm, yum.*

'Good,' Stella says, 'we need your help.' She nods toward the cheese and fruit.

Sam winks at me. 'Nice flowers, Willa. How was school?'

'So far, so good. Hey, Sam, there's a closed sign on the Library.'

Sam nods. 'Budget problems. The council's talking about curtailing non-essential services—'

'Non-essential services! The library isn't a non-essential—'

'OK, Willa,' Stella interrupts. 'What's essential right now is making dinner.'

There's a watering can on the floor by the door. I fill it and stick the flowers in. An orange barn cat stares up at the sunny faces and then nestles underneath. *The library is too an essential service.* I grab an oatmeal cookie and a glass of milk and begin slicing the cheddar cheese. I tell them about being elected Community Service Leader and how Tina and I are thinking of planning a little party on Halloween . . .

'Well,' Stella says, looking at Sam. 'That was quite a day you had, Willa. Any chance you squeezed in some Algebra?'

I change knives and start slicing the apples.

Sam laughs. 'I'm proud of you, Willa, about

the service thing. A college professor called it "Community rent". How we all have an obligation to pay rent: some of our time or talent or treasure – otherwise known as money – to help others.'

Stella looks up when Sam says 'money'.

'So what are you planning to do?' Sam asks.

'We haven't decided yet.' I arrange the fruit and cheese on a platter and open a box of crackers. 'But Tina and I were thinking if we got the class together on Halloween we could start brainstorming ways to serve—'

'Right now it's time to serve our *guests*,' Stella announces, standing up. 'You take the cheese, Willa. I've got the quiche.'

I knew this wasn't going to be simple.

3

The Honey-Do List

'So so' is good, very good,
very excellent good;
and yet it is not;
it is but so so.

– 'Silly Will' Shakespeare, *As You Like It*

We set the hors d'oeuvres on the table. Stella turns on some jazz, *'Come away with me . . .'* The sun is setting, painting our porch with the rich warm colour of honey.

I hear our new guests before I see them.

'Add that to the list, Papa B.'

'Come again, Chickles?'

'That sweet word thingamajinny they've got out front there.' The tall plump lady is pointing to my Bramble Board. 'I want one on our front lawn.'

'Right away, Mama B,' the man nods, fetching a notebook from his jacket. His jacket is purple with yellow paisley swirls. You don't see a lot of jackets like that on Cape Cod. And he has shoes to match.

'Make that *all* our front lawns,' the lady says, swooping back her boa. A purple feather flies off and lands on the cheddar cheese.

'Good, honey,' the man says, fumbling for his notebook again. 'Got it right here on the honey-do list. I'll do it soon as we get home.'

'Welcome to Bramblebriar,' Stella says, rising to the occasion. 'Such a pleasure to meet you. I'm Stella. You met my husband, Sam. This is our daughter, Willa.'

'Willa, say hello to Mr and Mrs Blazer. You'll know them from their company name, Blazer Buick USA. We've seen their commercials on TV.'

Actually, Stella hardly lets me watch TV, but you'd have to be a hermit crab not to have heard that annoying commercial: *Blazin', blazin', it's amazin'* . . .

The Blazers look at each other and then laugh like twins with a secret.

'Ready, Mama B?' Mr Blazer clears his throat.

'Ready, Papa B.' Mrs Blazer flips her boa.

*'Blazin', blazin', it's amazin', cars and trucks from
    coast to coast,*
*blazin', blazin', it's amazin', please excuse us while we
    boast,*
*Blazin', blazin', it's amazin', Blazer Buick sells
    the . . .'*

And not only are the Blazers belting it on Broadway, but they've got Macarena-style moves to go with it. *Oh, where's Sam?* I wish he could see this. I dig my fingernails into my palms to keep from giggling. The other guests stare speechless.

Stella nudges me.

I extend my hand. 'It's a pleasure to meet you, Mrs Blazer.'

'Oh, don't mind us,' she says, giggling. She grabs my hand and shakes it like she's pumping for oil. 'Call me Chickles or Mama B. Everybody does.'

As I shake I can't help noticing the diamond necklace, shaped like a limousine, parked over Mama B's amazing cleavage.

'My, aren't you a pretty little thing?' she says, looking me up and down.

Instinctively I stick out my chest and stand up straighter.

'And I'm Bellford T.' He shakes my hand. 'Papa B to friends like you. And yes, Mama, she's pretty as a picture.' He pats his heart. 'Makes me miss our Jubilee.'

There are cars and trucks on Papa B's tie, Buicks I assume and, as he pats his heart, the diamonds on his steering-wheel-shaped tie tack twinkle, *beep, beep, beep.*

'Is Jubilee your daughter?' Stella asks.

The Blazers nod, looking misty-eyed.

'Well, isn't that a lovely name,' Stella says. 'Jubilee.'

'That's actually her middle name,' Mama B clarifies. 'Her full name is Suzanna Jubilee, for it was truly a jubilee the day she was born.' Mama B sits down, swooshes her boa and settles her hands on her lap. She's gearing up for a long one.

'You see, I'd been labouring through that horrible hurricane, "Hoover", you remember the one . . .'

Stella is nodding like, *Yes, of course, how could anyone forget* . . .

'The power was out for days and the sky was dark as the devil, and every contraction was a dagger slicing through my . . .'

OK, way too much information.

'. . . but at the very moment our sweet Suzanna was born,' Mama B pauses for a sniffle – 'all I can say is, the sun shone through like it just learned how to shine.'

'That's right,' Papa B testifies with a hiccup, gazing upwards at the sky.

I look up too, half expecting to see angels waving down from the clouds. A fat gull swoops by, *caw*, and poops. I dig my nails deeper to keep from giggling. I have a bad habit of laughing when it's not appropriate. I wait to see if Stella will slip and say something sarcastic. That's my mother's bad habit.

But no, Stella's smiling and shaking her head from side to side, listening as if this is the most fascinating story ever. 'Well, we'd love to meet Suzanna Jubilee,' she says. 'The next time you come for a visit, you'll have to bring her.'

'You read my mind, Mrs Gracemore,' Mama B says. 'I was just saying as much to Papa. We'd have brought Suzy-Jube this time, but she's in the quarter-finals for Miss Daisydew and she's got an important session with her talent-trainer today.'

I'm dying to ask what Suzy-Jube's talent is, but Stella gives me the homework signal and I dutifully head up to my room. I need to stay on Stella's good side so I can pop the barn question tonight. Thankfully, now that Sam is in the picture, Stella has eased up on 'the rules' a bit, but homework hours are carved in stone.

After dinner I clear the dishes and help Bobbie and Makita set up the tables in the sunroom for breakfast. Later, I hear Stella and Sam talking in their room.

'They're loaded,' Stella says. 'They're staying until after Halloween and then they're coming back for Thanksgiving with a ton of relatives. They've reserved ten rooms, three suites and all the cottages and—'

I knock and Stella calls 'come in' in a chip-chippery voice. When business is good, Stella is good. Stella pays the bills at the Bramblebriar Inn.

She handles bookings and manages the staff. Sam's in charge of the kitchen and grounds. I do the games room and the Bramble Board and help with meals. And, whenever there's a wedding, Stella lets me assist. Stella used to be the Cape's most famous wedding planner, but now that she and Sam are married, she prefers a less stressful life. Running an Inn is challenging, but much easier than dealing with demanding debutantes.

'I finished all my homework, the Biology lab and extra-credit Algebra and I even started studying for the history quiz next week.'

'Excellent,' Stella says, pleased, but not really listening.

'So is it OK to have that Halloween community-service get-together?'

Sam nods at me and winks. Sam was a teacher. He's no dummy. He knows there are a few lines missing in the story. But, like always, Sam-the-man stands by me.

'Fine,' Stella says with a smile. Clearly her mind is elsewhere. She doesn't ask a million questions or even ask Sam for his opinion. 'Just let us know what you need.'

'Thanks, Mom. Thanks, Sam.'

Yes. I run before Stella changes her mind.

There's only one page left in my favourite journal. It's brown with a yellow sunflower on the cover. Gramp Tweed gave it to me on the worst day of my life. One of Stella's celebrity weddings had ended disastrously because of a foolish mistake by me. A soap star sued her. It made national news. Stella was angry and humiliated, and that, combined with her being scared to death over falling in love with Sam, was more than she could handle. She put our house on the market and whisked us off to Maine. That day we left Bramble and all the people I loved, somehow Gramp Tweed knew this blank book was just what I needed. I nearly missed my whole eighth-grade year before Stella came to her senses and we came home. This journal was a lifesaver during that long miserable year. I wrote and wrote, every feeling I was feeling, and every day I felt a little better.

I open the cover and read Gramp's inscription: 'To my kindred spirit, Willa . . . Remember to keep reading the best books while you are young . . .

And then someday, Willa, when you write your own, as I am certain you will, remember what Jo learns in *Little Women*. The secret is to write the truth and put your heart into it.'

I don't want to get my hopes up, but JFK's back and he's coming to the party in the barn. I don't know how 'compatible' we are, but even when gorgeous Tina was talking to him, he kept looking at me . . .

I can't believe Mum had a boyfriend. I hope she'll write to him. Mum deserves every speck of happiness . . .

What should we do for community service? Nana supports Bramble Head Start for kids. Sam stocks the Food Pantry with fresh produce. Stella runs races to raise money for the heart association. Mum said to pick a cause I care about . . .

When I finish writing, I hide my journal where a certain snooper won't find it.

There's a stack of library books on my night-stand. Two are due back tomorrow. I can't wait to ask Mrs Saperstone what's going on. I reread the first page of *The Great Gilly Hopkins*. It's going on my 'Willa's Pix' recommended list of books.

They say you can't judge a book by its cover, but I think you can by its first page. I liked Gilly from the go.

The second book is an old edition of *A Tale of Two Cities,* by Charles Dickens. The jacket is frayed and the top corners of pages are creased from readers marking their places over the years. The opening line is famous: '*It was the best of times, it was the worst of times . . .*' I sniff the book and smile. New books smell like ink. Old books are more mysterious. But new or old, I love them.

All those years when Stella kept moving us, it was hard to make lasting friends. The friends in my books were always there.

When my head clunks down on Dickens, I turn off the light. The screen is dark and then the movie starts playing in my mind. JFK standing there with those dreamy blue eyes, that dimple to die for . . . Come on, Cupid. Move your butt.

4

Ruby and the Bramble Burners

She hath more hair than wit,
and more faults than hairs,
and more wealth than faults.

— **Shakespeare,** *The Two Gentlemen of Verona*

Sam slides the newspaper towards me at breakfast. 'It doesn't look good for the library,' he says. 'Harry Sivler says the debt may be insurmountable.' Harry Sivler is that obnoxious Ruby Sivler's father. He owns half the town of Bramble. Nana hates him. She says he's a 'new money wash-ashore, who won't stop until he's torn down every sweet Cape cottage and built a tacky trophy in its place.'

I read the article. They're cutting back hours to three days a week and are 'in discussion with two neighbouring towns about the possibility of merging . . .'

'They can't do that!' I say. My heart is pounding.

Stella comes in from her morning run, sweating, huffing. 'Look at the time,' she says to me. 'Hurry up, Willa. You'll be late.'

At our lockers I start to tell Tina about the library, but she interrupts. 'Let's get Ruby to help with the Halloween party,' she says. 'We only have two weeks, and she's got lots of experience. Remember the June Bug in seventh grade?'

I do not have fond memories of the Bug. I spent all evening waiting – but JFK never turned up.

'Besides, Willa, it's time you and Ruby buried the hatches and . . .'

'It's *hatchet,* Tina, but maybe you're right.'

Before I settled here in Bramble, Ruby and Tina were best friends.

'Hey, girls! What do you think?'

Tina and I swing around at the sound of Ruby's voice.

'*Ahhh!*' We gasp in unison.

Ruby has been transformed. Her hair is permed and poofed, and very, very *red*. Her lips and fingernails are on fire too, and she's sporting a flaming leather jacket that fits so tight her boobs jut out like volcanoes. Ruby's a red-headed Dolly Parton.

'Mommy and I went to Spangles for the weekend, our favourite spa in Boston. Daddy flew us over in the new CJ.' I'm assuming the CJ is a plane. Ruby flashes her fingers so we can admire her manicure.

'Oh, *so glam*,' Tina says.

'And Mommy's favourite yogi, Albee Senile, was there. At first I was like, "yawn, yawn, look at that scraggly old dinosaur", and then at satsang that night Senile started mumbling something about "blossoming, blossoming, letting your inner bud bloom . . ." and all of a sudden I had this, I don't know . . . *awakening* . . . sort of like I finally woke up. Right then and there I decided to break out and do something dramatic, you know, make a personal statement, something to demonstrate my passionate personality, and so I made an appointment at the salon and . . .'

I am absolutely without words. Tina manages another, 'Glam.'

The bell rings and Ruby reluctantly sheds her red leather, stuffs her backpack in her locker, checks her make-up in the mirror and slams the door shut.

I jump.

'And guess what?' Ruby says. 'Big news! Tanner McGee just winked at me in the hall and said, "See you at the game, Ruby." And I said, "OK, Tanner. See ya then." Our first conversation. And he knows my *name*!'

Tina's body stiffens. She folds her arms. Uh-oh.

Tina and I are painfully aware and constantly reminded that Ruby made the cheerleading squad. The Bramble Burners. Tina was tragically disappointed. I didn't try out. I'd rather play ball than bounce on the sidelines.

The Burners wear skintight matching tops and short red skirts. Their favourite cheer is 'hot, hot, hot'. *Puke, puke*. But wait, in a few weeks, when the weather gets colder, the Burners will be freezing their you-know-whats-off.

'And did you hear?' Ruby drones on. 'Joey Kennelly's back!'

Now Ruby's got my attention. Two for two. Ruby's on a roll.

'He's gotten taller and his hair is longer and curly now. And that dimple . . .'

His name is Joseph. JFK to me.

'I'm into older boys now, but Joey is still such a cutie . . .' Ruby rambles on.

I look at Tina. She looks at me. Tina sends me a raised eyebrow 'do we still ask her?' and I send her back a scrunched-nosed 'I don't know, what do you think?'.

Tina decides. That's one of the things I like best about her. She has no trouble making quick decisions. Tina was born without the worry gene. I got the giant size.

'Hey, Rube,' Tina says, 'we've got big news too. Willa's parents said we could have a Halloween party in the barn at the Inn. Want to help?'

'Oh, how sweet,' Ruby says, smiling at us like we're munchkins from Oz. She twirls a red curl. 'But the Burners are having a bonfire on the beach. All of the cute boys are coming and . . .'

'Not Joseph K —' I start, then stop.

'Oh, that's OK.' Ruby stares at me. 'I mean all the *big boys* are coming.'

'Well then, you'd better have lots of *big* marshmallows . . .' I start, but a ripple of giggles interrupts me. Two Bramble Burners are coming out of the bathroom.

'Got to go,' Ruby says, and rushes to catch them. 'Hey, girls, wait up!'

Tina and I watch the Burners play with Ruby's red curls, squealing their approval, doing their dumb club signal, shaking their butts, fingers crooked on their head, like devils. Puke, puke.

I give Tina some gummy bears. I toss the rest in my mouth and chew.

'So what,' Tina says. 'We don't need her, Willa. We'll plan a party that will make their stupid bonfire look like a Cub-Scout weenie roast. Got some paper?'

Does a fish have fins? I pull out a notebook and pen.

'OK, *one*. Food. You get Sam going on the grub. Stuff *boys* like . . . chicken wings, ribs, pizza, nachos . . .'

This is definitely not Bramble Inn cuisine, but Sam's a guy, he'll understand.

'*Two*. Decorations. I'll get my mother to send over Betty to sweep out the place and Daddy'll fork up funds for prizes.'

Tina and Ruby are rich. I don't hold it against them. Stella and I used to be sort of rich, too, back when she was a wedding planner, but now that we are innkeepers, and Sam's not so into making money, we're just regular people.

'*Three*.' Tina's on a roll. 'Entertainment. I bet Luke and Jessie would appreciate a barn gig. They usually play in garages.'

Luke and Jessie are the hottest boys in our class. They just started a band.

'They're not very good,' Tina says, 'but who cares, they're ice cream.'

'What?' I stop writing. 'What do you mean, *ice cream*?'

Tina smiles like Garfield the cat. 'I thought you'd like that. Willa the word-lover. You know how they say a cute guy is 'eye-candy'? Well, I invented 'eye-scream'. Get it? Eye-candy, eye-scream. Ice-cream's just as sweet as candy, right?'

'Right, Tina.' I'm digging my nails in. 'Good one.'

'You're not kidding it's good.' Tina flips her hair, end of story. 'I think I should get a patent on it or something.'

'Speaking of patents,' I say, 'how's your Aunt Amber's business doing?'

'Awesome. She's already talking about franchising. See, Willa, I told you. It's all about compatibility. I'm working on my own list of questions. How hard can it be? Anyway, Luke and Jessie's band pukes, but all the freshmen girls will come to see them. We should charge admission, five bucks or so, to pay them. Got that?'

'Yep,' I'm writing as fast as I can. If Tina's brain clicked like this in class, she'd be in honours. 'I'm good. Keep going.'

'OK, *four*, you plan the games, Willa. Some sort of Halloween stuff.'

'Like what?'

'I don't know. Use that wild imagination of yours, Willa. Just be sure they're *fun*. No word games or anything. Think fun. Fun, fun, fun.'

I'm going to have to work on that one.

'And don't worry –' Tina winks – 'I'll bring the right music for the last dance, when the party's over and it's getting late and all that's left is that stairway to heaven.'

'What?' I'm confused.

Tina's face takes on a dreamy glow. 'Tanner McGee may get lured off to that stupid bonfire, but I bet your boy will show up. Joey Kennelly's a team player.'

'What stairway to heaven?'

'Oh, Willa,' Tina says, shaking her head. 'You've got to ditch Shakespeare and get to the *movies* more often.'

I'm still in the dark.

'The *ladder*, Willa,' Tina says. 'In the barn. The ladder up to the loft.'

5

This Is America

Knowing I lov'd my books, he furnish'd me . . .
with volumes that I prize above my dukedom.

— The 'Bard of Avon', *The Tempest*

After school, I bike to the library. The sign is still up, the door is locked. I put Gilly and Dickens in the returns-box and walk around the back to the courtyard. The whale spoutin' fountain is off. The pennies are gone. I need to talk to Gramp.

The chimes overhead jingle as I enter Sweet Bramble Books. The smell of saltwater taffy makes me want to do a Snoopy dance. '*Mrrrrah*,' Muffles greets me from her perch in the window. I wonder what she's keeping warm today.

Gramp Tweed and I have this tradition. Every Friday he puts a new book for me on the window ledge. Muffles sits on the book, like a furry mother bird on an egg, until I arrive. 'Hey, Muffles.' I scratch her and she leaps, ever the coy cat. *A Tree Grows in Brooklyn*. I grab some fudge, plop on the couch, and open it. 'Serene was a word you could put to Brooklyn, New York. Especially in the summer of—'

'I'll be interested to hear what you think,' Gramp says, coming out of the Cape Cod Authors aisle with my Shakespeare teacher, Dr Swaminathan.

'Thank you, sir,' Swammy says. 'I appreciate your recommendations.'

When Swammy leaves, Gramp makes us some tea. Lemon, no sugar, the way we like it. 'Where's Nana, Gramp?'

'Out walking Scamp. I promised your Nana if she walks every day, I'll take her to New York City in December. Do you know she's never seen a Broadway show?'

I'm glad Nana's exercising. Her doctor changed her heart medication again and said to lose some weight.

'What do you know about the library, Gramp?'

'Nothing's been decided yet. It's on the agenda next council meeting.'

'Can kids talk at that meeting?'

'Well, you have to be eighteen to vote, but there's no rule against talking. This is Cape Cod. First place the pilgrims stopped, freedom of expression and all that . . .'

'Great,' I say. 'I've got an expression for that council.' I get up to leave. 'Thanks for the book, Gramp. It looks good. Tell Nana I said hello.'

'Wait, Willa. Your candy.' Gramp comes towards me with a bag.

That's the other Friday tradition. Candy.

Books and candy. What's a weekend without them?

I head towards the beach eating Swedish fish, but then something tells me to try the library again. It's getting windy anyway, feels like it might rain.

The old brick building looks deserted. Green ivy hands wave sadly in the wind, *Willa, Willa, Willa.* I stare at the sign on the door.

That door seemed so heavy when I was a little girl, but I always insisted on opening it myself.

Summer was Stella's busiest wedding season and so she'd ship me here to stay with Nana on the Cape. Nana had the story-time schedule posted on the refrigerator and we'd go to every one.

Mrs Saperstone would dress like characters in the books and surprise us with treats, like honey on scones the time we read *The Bee Tree*. It was always so much fun. After, Nana and I would walk out to the courtyard and I'd pat the smooth back of the big grey whale. I'd close my eyes and make a wish and toss a penny in the water.

And I'll never forget the day I got my own library card. Mrs Saperstone presented it like it was a college diploma. I checked out twelve books, 'the limit for a new patron', and Nana took me for ice cream to celebrate, but I couldn't wait to get home and read. No way are they closing my library.

That's it. That's what we'll do. We'll save the Bramble Library.

Just then, the door opens. Mrs Saperstone steps out. I can't wait to tell her.

She starts slowly down the stairs, a bag of books in each hand. She once said she reads three a day so she 'won't miss any good ones'. Although she's probably older than Nana, Mrs Saperstone is always so excited talking about books, she always looks young to me. Until today. Today Mrs Saperstone looks old. There's a swathe of grey hair on her forehead and dark circles under her eyes.

'Hi, Mrs Saperstone. I'm glad you're here.'

'Hello, Willa.' Her face brightens. She sets her bags down. The tan one says 'Librarians are Booked for Life'. The green one says 'Got Books, Let's Read!'. She notices *A Tree Grows in Brooklyn*. 'Good choice,' she says.

'Gramp picked it out for me.'

'Well, at least I know Alexander will point the good ones your way. You always were one of my best customers, Willa.'

'Don't worry, Mrs Saperstone. I've got a plan.'

Mrs Saperstone pulls a piece of lint from her coat. She fixes the yellow scarf around her neck. She doesn't look at me. 'I think it's a done deal, Willa.'

'No,' I say so loudly that it startles Mrs Saperstone. 'I won't let it happen.'

Mrs Saperstone looks quickly at me, then away. She clears her throat. 'No, Willa. I'm certain the council will sell the building. The roof is leaking, the brick is crumbling. We need a complete technology upgrade . . .'

'*But what about the books?*'

Mrs Saperstone squeaks. 'I'm done battling, Willa.' She picks up *Brooklyn*, then drops it. 'The council's making arrangements with another town to . . .'

'No. That's not right.' My heart is pounding. 'This is Bramble's library. These are Bramble's books. And what about *you*. Where will *you* go?'

Mrs Saperstone squawks like a gull caught in a net. I'm afraid she might start sobbing, so I stop. 'Don't worry, Mrs Saperstone. I won't let them close our library. I'll go to the meeting . . .'

It starts pouring as I bike home. I stop and put *Brooklyn* in my backpack. I think how, if the book got ruined, Gramp would just order me another. I'm lucky to have a bookstore in the family. But not everybody can afford every book they want to read. That's what libraries are for. Aren't libraries a constitutional right or something? What's wrong with that stupid council anyway? This is America.

At home I go online and start searching. I download every article I can find on the importance of libraries. I find that Bramble isn't the only town where a library is in trouble. It seems stupidity is spreading. What will they close next? *Schools?*

6

Trick or Treat

Double, double toil and trouble;
Fire burn, and cauldron bubble . . .

— **Shakespeare, Macbeth**

'Trick or treat!'

Tina's a genie. I'm a chef and already regretting it. It seemed like a good idea this morning, but now that I see Tina, I wish I picked something prettier.

JFK is coming to the party.

We weren't going to dress up, but then Stella insisted we had to wear costumes if we were going to 'ring people's doorbells begging for candy'. So we told everybody there would be a contest for best costume. Tina's father came through with prizes.

When Tina comes to get me, Stella is ladling out hot mulled cider for our guests on the porch, wearing her tall black witch's hat. Stella has two Halloween costumes. One year she's the Cat in the Hat. The next year she's a witch. Cat, witch, cat, witch. That's all I'm going to say.

Main Street is packed with ghosts and goblins and superheroes of every sort. Friends from our class wave from across the street. Trish is a lion. Kelsey's a scarecrow. Emily's covered in tin foil.

'I think they're from *The Wizard of Oz*,' Tina says.

'Hey, girls!' Two more friends, Lauren and Alexa, call to us. All the freshmen girls are coming to the barn party. We see some guys from our class, but no JFK yet.

Bramble knows how to do holidays. The hardware store, florist, card shop, fish market, pharmacy, cinema, every restaurant and clothing store, even the tourist places, are dressed for Halloween. And no store does it better than Sweet Bramble Books.

'There's our girl!' Nana's a black-and-yellow-striped bumblebee with two blinking bobble things on her head. She's weighing penny candy for a customer. Scamp bounds over to say hello. When I squat down, he licks my face, then rolls on his back so I'll scratch his belly. Wizard Gramp waves from the book register. He's wearing a purple robe and a tall pointed cap covered with silver stars. Muffles drags her eyes away from the show outside for a quick *mrrrah*.

'Trick or treat!'

Nana finishes and flies toward us, '*Buzzzzzzzz*.' Tina steps back.

'Here, try this, Willa.' Nana hands me a piece of black saltwater taffy. She has me test out all her new flavours. She's trying to retain her 'Best Sweets on the Upper Cape' award in *Cape Cod Life* magazine. The competition is tough. Cape Cod's loaded with great candy stores.

I pop it in and start to chew. I'm expecting black liquorice, but it's lemon, *sour lemon*, so sour it's making my tongue curl. '*Yuck*, Nana. What's this?'

'*Trick* or treat,' Nana says, laughing. 'Sorry, sweetie, I couldn't resist. Pretty clever for an old bat, I mean *bee*, huh?'

'Hysterical, Nana.'

Tina tugs on my arm, 'Come on, Willa. We've got to go. It's almost eight.'

'Here, Willa,' Nana says, 'we made these up specially for you and your friends.' She hands us each a fat orange bag full of candy. It feels like it weighs two pounds.

'Thank you!' Tina says, and gives Nana a hug.

'Can I have an extra one?' I ask Nana quietly.

Nana smiles, but doesn't snoop. Stella's snoopy enough for the whole family.

We hear the Buoy Boys warming up as we reach the Inn. They started out as the Beach Boys, but Luke's mother, who's a lawyer, said that name was taken and she didn't want to get sued. So the Beaches became the Buoys.

'Oh God, they sound awful,' Tina says.

The labyrinth, the circular garden maze behind the Inn, looks especially awesome tonight. The labyrinth is Sam's baby. He planted perennial flowers and bushes all along the winding pathway so that, no matter what the season, there's always something colourful to see. Our guests enjoy walking the labyrinth for its peaceful effect, but for tonight, Sam-the-man turned it into a 'Circle of Scares, Enter if You Dare'. You have to walk through it to get to the party in the barn.

Sam strung white netting across the labyrinth path, attaching it to the tops of cornstalks, creating a cobweb roof. Wet spaghetti hair and Jell-O eyeball booby traps are set to plop down in your face and there are secret spots where creatures leap out at you, screaming bloody murder. And, being the poet that he is, Sam made grave markers with creepy quotes from Edgar Allan Poe and Shakespeare, like 'Eye of newt, and toe of frog, Wool of bat, and tongue of dog.'

Macbeth may be lost on some, but I appreciate the literary allusions.

'Hey, Willa. Hey, Tina.' All the girls are starting to arrive, mostly freshmen, some sophomores. Tina and I are sitting at a table at the entrance to the barn. I keep watching for JFK. It's getting chilly. I'm glad I'm a chef. Tina's shivering in her chiffon. We put the five dollar admission fees into the glass jar and say, 'Have fun.'

The Buoy Boys sound like foghorns, but they could be lip-syncing snow and it wouldn't matter.

The girls are knocking each other over to get in closer. Tina used to have a crush on Jessie, before Tanner McGee. JFK, where are you?

Sam sneaks by us quietly to check the warming trays under the food. He gives me a thumb's up. 'All set, Willa? Have fun.'

'Thanks, Sam.'

Next, Stella stomps up. 'Keep the volume down, girls. Some guests might be trying to sleep. And don't forget it's over at ten, Willa, and I mean ten. Not a minute—' Just then the Blazers appear.

'Can we join in?' Mama B asks, a giant pumpkin in orange boas.

Tina kicks me under the table.

'Been years since the prom,' Papa B says, in black cape and top hat – a vampire, I think.

'Why, certainly.' Stella changes faces in a flash. 'Isn't this fun? A party in the barn! Makes you feel like a kid again, doesn't it?'

Papa B sticks a rolled-up bill in the jar.

'Oh, no, that's OK,' I say. 'You're our guests.'

'We insist,' Mama B says, giggling and grabbing Papa B's hand. 'Come on, Bellford, let's shake a leg.'

Oh gosh, how embarrassing . . . .

And then I see him.

JFK.

He's walking through the 'Circle of Scares, Enter if You Dare', and he's smiling like he's having fun. Yeah, Sam. Thanks, Sam.

JFK's even got a costume on. He's a chef too.

'Ooh, looks like somebody's *compatible*.' Tina kicks me again.

'*Shhhh*.' I kick her back. 'He's almost here.'

Breathe, Willa, Breathe.

7

The Party in the Barn

If music be the food of love, play on . . .
— **'Shake-it, Will' Shakespeare**, *Twelfth Night*

Just as JFK reaches us, Tina says, 'To pee or not to pee, that is the question.'

'*What!?*'

'Got to go, Willa.' Tina laughs and leaves.

'Tina, wait.' But she's gone.

'Hi, Joseph,' I manage to say. 'Thanks for coming.'

'So what do you like to cook?' he says.

'What?'

'You're a chef, right?' JFK smiles. There's that dimple. My head fills with fog.

'Oh, right. Nothing, really. Tuna fish is about the extent of my talent.'

JFK nods in towards the party. 'Do they rot or what?' He laughs.

'Oh, they're OK,' I say. 'Besides, they're eye – yaaffordable.'

JFK peers into the dark barn. I peer into his ocean eyes and start to sail away.

'Willa, my darling, dance with me?'

'*What?!*' I swerve back to shore.

JFK laughs. 'I said, "Willa, I'm starving, what's there to eat."'

'Oh, sure, come on.' I push the admission jar forward so people will see it. All the freshmen girls are here now anyway and I have a fishy feeling the rest of the boys got lured to the Burners' bonfire.

JFK and I fill our plates and sit down on a bale of hay. The Buoys are playing a decent song and all the girls are dancing. Tina's flirting with Jessie. So much for Tanner McGee. I hope JFK doesn't feel weird being the only boy here besides the Buoys, but he doesn't seem to mind.

'The wings are good,' he says.

'Thanks, I'll tell my dad Chef Kennelly approves.'

Joseph laughs and takes off his tall white hat.

He smooths his hair. It did get curly while he was away, or maybe it's being back in the ocean air.

I take off my chef's hat, and smooth my hair too. I wish I had a mirror. I probably have hat hair. 'How does your father like his new job?'

'He loves it.' JFK tries Sam's nacho supremos. Taco chips smothered with salsa, meat and cheese. 'These are awesome.' He wipes his mouth.

'Glad you like them,' I say. He has beautiful lips.

'Yeah, my dad always wanted to run the *Cape Cod Times*. It was his big dream.'

'Good for him. I think it's great when people's dreams come true.' Oh, no, I sound like Pollyanna. Oh, so what, Willa. That girl always gets a bad rap. All she was trying to do was make the world a happier—

'Hey, I made the Bucks,' Joseph says. 'Second string, quarterback.'

Oh no, soccer I know. Football's a foreign planet. 'That's great. Congratulations.'

'You like football?'

'I love it.' You are such a liar, Willa.

JFK's face brightens. 'Looking good for the Pats, huh?'

The New England Patriots, football team. Sam said even if you hate sports, there are two teams every Cape Codder absolutely must know. The Boston Red Sox, baseball, and the New England Patriots, football. Thanks, Sam.

'Yeah, they're looking great,' I say. Mental note, start reading the sports page. 'The Pats are my favourite team.' Remember Pinocchio, Willa.

'What book are you reading now?' JFK asks. 'I always see you reading.'

How sweet of him to change the subject to something I'm interested in.

'I just finished *A Tale of Two Cities* and I'm starting *A Tree Grows in Brooklyn*. Are you reading anything?'

'Well, Shakespeare, like everybody. And I'm still trying to finish *Moby Dick*. I promised my father. But right now I'm into *The Outsiders*. It's good.'

He reads for pleasure. This is great.

'What's the best book you've ever read?' I ask.

'I don't know,' JFK says. 'That's hard to say. I have a lot of fav—'

There's an ear-splitting laugh. The Blazers are in the horse stall next to us, dancing to a different drum indeed. Papa B spins Mama out like a yo-yo, then snaps her back into his arms. She gives him a big slurpy kiss and they laugh like looney birds.

'Sorry,' I say to JFK. 'They're our new guests.'

'That's OK.' JFK laughs. 'They're having fun.'

The Buoys take a break. Tina turns on some music. It's a favourite of mine. I think about dancing. I'd love to dance. 'What kind of music do you like, Joseph?'

'Rap.'

Oh no, I'm more of a top-forty girl. 'What do you like about it?'

'I like the beat. How it flows. It's like poetry except it's music.'

Wow, that's beautiful.

JFK talks about different rap artists. 'I'm into the Lyricists,' he says.

I try to remember the names so I can check them out when I get home.

'Too bad about the library, huh?' JFK is looking at me.

'What?'

'I know that's one of your favourite places. I've seen you there a few times.'

Just then I remember seeing JFK at the library once too. He was writing at the table by the grandfather clock in the upstairs Reading Room. He nodded at me, but went right back to his writing. I wonder if he was working on lyrics. 'Yes,' I say, 'I heard they're thinking of closing it—'

'No,' JFK says, 'they're definitely closing it. It's decided. Dad said it will be on the front page tomorrow.'

'What?' My heart is pounding. 'They can't do that! Why? When?'

'Whoa, Willa. Hold on.' JFK is laughing. 'You'd make a good reporter.'

'They can't close our library.'

'I know. That would be bad,' JFK says. 'I like the old place too. But my Dad says it costs a fortune to run. It needs a new roof, new heating system, tons of stuff.'

'But the library is a Bramble landmark, a historic—'

'I know, but it's all about the money.'

'How much money?'

'I don't know,' JFK says. 'I'll get more details from my father. But, hey, listen, we can't save the library tonight.'

We head to the dessert table. Sam spent all day baking chocolate cupcakes and orange-frosted cookies, pumpkin and apple pies. We both reach for the cider doughnuts, sugar-coated and still warm.

'These are my favourite,' I say.

'Mine too.'

JFK is staring at my lips. He's leaning forward. Oh no.

'You've got some sugar there.' He brushes it away.

Boing. Bullseye, Cupid. Something flutters up near the hayloft. Could be the fat baby himself. More likely a barn bat.

'Sorry, Joey,' Tina says, pulling my arm. 'I've got to borrow Willa.'

Talk about terrible timing.

'Let's bob for apples, kiddies,' Tina announces.

The kiddies groan. Nobody wants to bob.

'We're in high school,' somebody shouts.

'Willa's dad put quarters in them,' Tina says, 'silver dollars too.'

Still no takers.

'I'll go,' JFK says. What a good sport. He kneels by the large silver tub on the floor. Fat red apples are floating in the water.

'Hands behind your back, Joey,' Tina says, looking at her stopwatch. 'You've got thirty seconds. Ready, set, *go*.'

JFK opens his mouth wide and tries clamping his teeth around one of the apples. It's harder than it looks. The apples are bobbing and JFK's chomping like an alligator, getting wet, laughing, snorting. 'I've got water up my nose.'

The girls are crowding around. Tina starts the count, 'Ten, nine . . .'

Joseph gets an apple and then another one before Tina yells, 'Stop.'

Later I ask the Blazers if they'll be the honorary judges for the costume contest.

'We'd be tickled pink,' Chickles says, all flushed from dancing. She wipes her forehead with a handkerchief and swipes her boa back. Bellford blows his nose and fixes his tie. They circulate the room, asking questions, taking notes.

'Suzy-Jube would love this,' Bellford says. 'She's great with costumes.'

I can't wait to meet that girl. I hope she comes at Thanksgiving.

The judges retire to their horse stall to confer.

'And the winner is . . . the Wizards of Oz!'

Trish, Kelsey and Em start clapping, all excited. Tina gives them prizes.

'Next up is the scavenger hunt,' I say. Sam and I hid plastic spiders and chicken bones splattered with red paint. It seemed like fun at the time.

It doesn't now. I pass out the lists of things to hunt for. 'Break up into teams of three or four and—' Nobody is paying attention.

'Willa,' Tina says, pointing up. 'Listen.'

There's a faint tapping on the old metal roof. *Tink, tink . . . tink, tink, tink . . .* then louder and louder. Rain.

Tina winks at me, points at JFK, and then subtly nods towards the hayloft.

No, I shake my head. Batwings are fluttering in my stomach.

'One last dance, kiddies,' Tina announces.

The music starts. 'And they're buy-uy-ing the Stair-air-way to Hca – ven.'

JFK is walking towards me. The bats are beating bongos now.

No, it can't be. I look away, then back again.

It's true. He's getting closer and closer. I can't hear the music any more. He's reaching out his hand. He's going to ask me to—

'OK, party's over,' Stella cackles, swooping in like Darth Vader, still wearing her witch's hat. 'It's quarter after ten.'

In a nanosecond Stella's mega-mother-radar registers my exact location. She looks at me and then at JFK, then at me, then at JFK.

He sticks his hands in his pockets. I check my face for sugar.

Stella moves towards me, I'm melting, melting . . . then she remembers her mission and turns. 'Who needs a ride?' she says. 'It's pouring out there. Mr Gracemore and I can each take five or so. Here's a phone if you need to call your parents.'

Talk about raining on someone's stairway.

'I'll come by tomorrow morning to help clean up,' Tina says.

'Thanks, Willa,' JFK says, chef's hat in hand. 'It was fun.'

He's gone before I can give him the two-pound bag of candy.

8

A Beach Day

Shall I compare thee to a summer's day?
Thou art more lovely and more temperate.

– Shakespeare, *Sonnet 18*

Great party. I take off my chef's costume and stare at myself in the mirror. Still skinny as a Pixy Stick, but getting some curves. Eyes, blue, my best feature. Hair, like a horsetail, worst feature. The style was good at first. Ruby actually suggested it, she has a flair for hair, but I'm ready for a change. Maybe I'll ask her.

Ruby is annoying, but I blame a lot on her mother. Stella can be a pain in the brain, but I wouldn't want Sherry Sivler for a mother. Mrs Sivler actually wore pink satin pants and a mink-edged pink leather jacket to BUC last weekend.

Puke, puke. She honk-talks like a foghorn and wears so much make-up that little kids could learn their colours from her face. I see pink, red, purple . . . Maybe I'll get my hair curled.

I look at the photographs on my dresser. Stella, Nana, and the men in my life. My birth father, Billy Havisham. Mother says I have his eyes. Me and Gramp Tweed back when he was just 'Mr Tweed' at the Father-Daughter Pancake Breakfast. Sam in his favourite fisherman's sweater. Soon maybe another handsome face. *JFK*.

I put on my pyjamas and snuggle. I open *A Midsummer Night's Dream*, then close it. Tonight I'm in the mood for a movie. I close my eyes and there it is. The Halloween Party in the barn. JFK in a chef's hat, walking out of the labyrinth, smiling. The two of us talking about books and rap. 'It's like poetry except it's music.' We both like cider doughnuts. Talk about being compatible. And those sea-blue eyes, those dreamy brown curls. What's that Shakespeare line about a summer's day? JFK is more beautiful than that. JFK's a beach day. He's walking towards me slowly, staring into my eyes, reaching out his hand . . . 'And they're buy-uy-ing the Stair-air-way to Hea—'

My bedroom door opens. *Poof* goes the movie. Stella is standing there.

'And so what did your class decide on?'

'What? How about knocking, Mother?'

'I did.' Stella shakes her sleek black hair, still wet from the rain. Other mothers might look like drowned rats right about now. Even soaked, Stella is stunning.

'We got your friends all home safely,' she says, still by the door.

I yawn. 'Good, thanks.' I yawn again as if I'm about to fall asleep.

But Stella's on a mission. 'So what volunteer thing did you decide on?'

'What?'

'Wasn't that the purpose for the party? To plan your service project?'

'Oh, right.' *Come on, Willa, think.* 'We talked about a lot of stuff.'

Stella walks to my desk. She picks up a notebook. History. Easy. I could get an A in my sleep. I'm so bored in class I doodle. *Oh no, the*

Cupids. Stella's staring at the flying babies. 'And who was that boy I saw you talking to?'

Something snaps inside. 'The library.'

'What?' Stella veers off course.

'That's what we're going to do. We're saving the Bramble Library.'

'What? How?' Stella starts. Now she sounds like a reporter.

'That's quite a project,' Sam says from the doorway. 'May I come in?'

'Sure.'

Sam puts his arm around Stella's shoulder and kisses her on the cheek. He sits on the edge of my bed. Stella leans against my desk with her arms folded.

'Joseph Kennelly's dad said it will be on the front page tomorrow.'

Sam nods. 'I heard they met in a closed session today.'

Stella looks bored.

'They can't make a decision like that in private,' I say.

'If there's another meeting,' Sam says, 'maybe your class could attend and—'

'It's a money matter, I'm sure,' Stella says, standing up. Sam and I can always count on Stella for the financial viewpoint.

'I think it's admirable that your class wants to tackle such a big issue,' Sam says. 'But I imagine they are talking a lot of money.'

'Well, we'll figure out something.' I am feeling confident at the moment. Tina and I just pulled off an awesome party. 'Where there's a will there's a way, right?'

'Speaking of Will,' Sam says. He runs his hand over the thick black *Complete Works of Shakespeare* on my nightstand. 'What are you reading next?'

Sam is a great innkeeper, but I know he misses teaching. Sam was the best English teacher I've ever had. Although I must say Swammy is no swimmy minnow.

'*A Midsummer Night's Dream.*'

'Nice,' Sam says. His face lights up. 'Aren't Quince and Bottom hysterical?'

'Speaking of dreams,' Stella interrupts, 'time for bed, Willa. Rosie's got a family wedding and Daryl called in sick, so you and I are on breakfast duty.'

'OK, sure. I'll set my alarm.'

After they kiss me goodnight and leave, I lie there thinking about how to save the library. How I'm definitely going to talk at that meeting. I look over at my stack of library books. I pick up *The Education of Little Tree*. Mrs Saperstone recommended it. '*Gramma said when you come on something good, first thing to do is share it with whoever you find; that way, the good spreads out . . .*' Mrs Saperstone always knows the good books. Mum says I'm a matchmaker. Librarians are matchmakers too. They match kids with books.

No way are they closing my library.

I'm wide awake now. I pick up old Will and find my place in *A Midsummer Night's Dream*. The language is so beautiful. The sounds roll off my tongue: '. . . *once I sat upon a promontory, and heard a mermaid on a dolphin's back uttering such dulcet and harmonious breath that the rude sea grew civil at her song and certain stars shot madly from their spheres, to hear the sea-maid's music . . .*'

So lyrical, so poetic. I wonder how Shakespeare would sound in rap?

'It's like poetry except it's music,' JFK had said.

9

Ben Franklin

Be not afraid of greatness:
Some are born great, some achieve greatness,
And some have greatness thrust upon them.

— **Shakespeare**, *Twelfth Night*

I'm up early. There's much to do. I help Stella make apple muffins and cut vegetables for the omelettes. Outside, the sun is shining. I sweep leaves off the front-porch steps and get the letters I need to change the Bramble Board. 'B, E, N, O, T . . .' I notice the cherry tree I planted when we first moved in is finally starting to grow.

'Good morning, Willa,' Mama B calls out. The Blazers are heading up the driveway, in matching pink velour warm-up suits, all rosy-cheeked from their walk.

'We wanted to thank you again, honey, for a lovely evening.'

'I'm glad you had a good time.'

'When's the next dance party?' Papa B asks.

'Oh, that was the only one.'

'No.' Chickles's chin drops. 'I was just telling Papa I hoped you'd have another for Thanksgiving. We had so much fun, didn't we, Bell? More fun than the time—'

'Willa!' Stella shouts from inside.

Thanks, Stella. Saved by the yell.

'I'm sorry, but I've got to go. Mother and I are on breakfast duty.'

'Certainly, honey,' Mrs Blazer says. 'You run right along.'

Phew. I hurry in and wash my hands.

'Here, take the honeydews,' Stella says. She adjusts a few of the strawberry garnishes and hands me the tray.

As I walk out to the breakfast porch I look at the green melons and giggle. I'm imagining Mama B saying, 'Put a barn in the backyard for dance parties on the honey-do list, Papa. No, make that barns for *all our backyards*.'

The Blazers are amazin'-ly rich. I overheard Stella telling Sam that they own four houses. The 'mother home', another on each coast, and a 'chateau d'amour' in France. Maybe they would make a donation to save the Bramble Li—

'What did you two chefs cook up last night?' Tina pops her head in through the window. 'Things looked pretty hot.'

'Shhhhh.' I look behind me for Stella. 'We had a nice talk. That's all.'

'Come on,' Tina teases. 'Dish it up, chef.'

'We had a nice talk. That's all.' We head out to the barn.

'I hope Ruby kept her red nails off Tanner last night,' Tina says.

'I wouldn't worry, Tina. The rain probably ruined the bonfire anyway . . .'

'Did you see *Jessie* last night?' Tina has already moved on.

'Well I certainly heard him.'

'Who cares if he can't play the guitar?' Tina says. 'His hair is so yummy. And that earring? He looks British or something, sort of a cross between Beckham and that hunk from the Harry Potter movies, or, maybe that boy from *Better Date Than Never*.'

I'm not following most of this, but I just nod along.

'Wait,' Tina says, 'hold everything. How much money did we make?'

'Let's check.' I unscrew the mayonnaise jar and empty it on the table.

Tina sees it first. 'A hundred bucks! Someone put in a *hundred bucks*.'

'Let me see. It was probably a trick.' Nope. That's Ben Franklin all right.

'Who would put in a hundred bucks?' Tina swipes Ben from my hand.

It's easy to connect the dots. 'The Blazers,' I say. 'Our new rich guests.'

'Wow,' Tina says, 'that was nice of them.'

'No, wait, Tina.' I take Ben back. 'I've got to give them change.'

'Why, Willa? They can read English, can't they? It said "five dollars" right on the jar. I'm sure they were just trying to support the cause.'

'What cause? We didn't say anything about a cause.'

'I know, Willa, but why spoil their fun? Let them feel proud about helping out the younger generation. You know, sort of like a community service.'

Tina's good, really good.

'No, Tina. It's not right. I have to at least offer them change.'

'Oh, all right, Willa.' Tina huffs. 'You're such a Goody-two-shoes. But don't twist their hammy arms too hard. If they say "keep it", let's keep it.'

Tina counts out the rest of the money. 'I'll pay the Buoys,' she says. 'It'll give me a reason to stop by Jessie's. And let's just split the rest. We did do all the work.'

After Tina leaves, I mix up some tuna, pack a lunch, and bike out to Sandy Beach. When I come up over the bluff, the wind whooshes hello and the waves swim in to meet me. I take a deep breath and smile.

At the bottom of the steps, I ditch my sneakers and sink my toes in the sand. *Hmmm*. Maybe the last barefoot day until spring. I walk out to the end of the jetty and back, then spread out my towel for lunch. A fat grey gull lands next to me.

He gives me a quick beady eye: 'Are you throwing me a crumb or what?'

I don't. He caws off, annoyed. Silly bird.

There are three sailboats out by Cotuit. I bite into a MacIntosh apple. JFK was such a good sport getting the bobbing going last night. I wipe the apple juice off my chin, remembering the feel of JFK's fingers as he brushed the sugar off my face.

After lunch, I walk along the ocean side of Poppy Spit, a narrow strip of beach, ocean on the right, bay on the left, about a mile long. Out near the end, there's an area they rope off to protect the nests of endangered birds. Tiny terns and piping plovers, crazy little endangered birds, are scampering ahead of me right now. Each time my dark shadow gets closer, they sweep up in a noisy flourish, fly up the beach a bit, then settle back on the sand. When they see me again, they swoop up again, playing the same game all over. Silly birds.

I start thinking about community service and the Bramble Library. Well, I've found a cause I care about. Hopefully my class will like the idea.

And how can we raise the money? And how much money do they need?

As I walk on, the wind and waves wash my worries away. Cool water laps against my feet. I keep my eyes open for beach glass and orange jingle shells.

We made money last night, more then we expected. And everybody had fun. Maybe we can do more events like that. Stella can't object to saving the library. And I'll have all those chances to be with JFK. That's it! Yes! *Thank you*.

I sprint around the tip of the Spit. Strong ocean currents converge with calm bay ones here, making a dangerous whirlpool. A boy drowned here once. I turn left, in towards the bay side, and stop. There's the spot where JFK and I sat on that magical day. He kissed me quickly on the cheek. He smelt like peppermint gum.

'*Caw, caw*,' a gull swoops in and another takes off like a relay. I head back down the beach. I saved the best part of lunch for last. Sam's famous chocolate-chip cookies with toffee candy-bar chunks. *Mmmm*.

There's a patch of rugosa by the steps. The

sweet-cinnamon-smelling pink beach roses grow wild all over the Cape. I pick one, probably the last of the season, and stick it in my hair. I wonder what JFK is doing today?

10

Ruby's Revelation

The web of our life is of a mingled yarn,
good and ill together.

— **Shakespeare, All's Well That Ends Well**

It's an 'outie', out-of-uniform day, in honour of the
annual Student-Faculty soccer game. Outie days
are causes for great rejoicing at Bramble Academy.
We get a chance to dress like ourselves and ditch
the drab uniforms.

I put on orange Bermudas and my favourite
striped rugby shirt. I grab a juice and a cranberry
muffin and bike to school early. No one is in
the hall when I tie the two-pounder on JFK's
locker.

Dear Joseph,
I meant to give this to you at the party. Thanks for coming.
It was fun.
    Willa

At lunch I tell Tina about my idea to hold events in the Inn barn to raise money for the library. Tina doesn't need two invitations for fun. 'Fun, fun, fun,' she says.

'Tanner McGee's a jerk,' Ruby announces, slamming down her books so hard my vegetable soup sloshes on the table. 'Lana Sharkey can have him.'

Lana Sharkey is a junior and the head of the Bramble Burners.

'Tanner was just sitting there on a log all by himself –'

I look to see if Tina is jealous – just a while ago she was making a list of all the ways she and Tanner were compatibly perfect – but no, Tina's stabbing her salad bowl. 'They're so stingy with the cheese around here,' she says.

'– and all I did,' Ruby rolls on, 'was sit next to Tanner and ask if I could roast him a hotdog or something and then, all of a sudden, Lana Sharkey comes running over all cat crazy and whispered something really mean to me, and then they got up and walked off together. Tanner didn't even wait for his hotdog.'

I'm dying to make eye contact with Tina, but she's still searching for cheese. Clearly she's over Tanner McGee. I guess it's all about Jessie now. Good. Jessie and JFK are friends. Maybe the four of us can . . .

'Anyway,' Ruby says, folding her arms. 'I thought about it all weekend. And I decided that Tanner was just using me to get back at Lana for flirting with that new transfer kid, Chris Ruggiero. Wow, have you seen him yet? What a beamer . . .'

I keep sipping my vegetable soup, not nearly as good as Sam's, but I'll deal – nodding like I'm listening, eyes on the door for JFK.

'At first I was hurt.' Ruby sighs again. 'But then I said to myself, "So what? Let it go," or as Yogi Senile would say, "Breathe and move mountains, breathe and move on." So I said to myself, "What's more important, Ruby Sivler? Fighting over a boy or being a *Bramble Burner*?" I don't need Lana

Sharkey mad at me. She's actually adding one of my moves to the new half-time cheer –'

I keep watching the door for JFK. I wonder what he thought of the candy. I wonder what his favourite candy is. I wonder what . . .

'– and so I decided . . .' Ruby's still talking. Tina clicks open her mirror and puts on lipstick. Ruby is annoyed that she doesn't have Tina's full attention. She clears her throat loudly. 'So, like I was saying. I decided Lana can have Tanner McGee. I'm going back with Joey Kennelly.'

'What?' Tina and I say with the timing of twins.

'What do you mean you're going back with Joey,' Tina says, looking quickly at me. 'When were you ever *with* Joey?'

The soup is swirling in my stomach. *It's not Joey. It's JFK. And he's mine.*

'Oh, come on,' Ruby squints at Tina. 'Don't you remember? Joey and I had a good thing going before he moved to Minnesota. We had some nice times together.'

What good thing? What nice times? Potatoes and carrots and celery are swirling.

'I'm definitely ready for older guys,' Ruby says. 'But Joey is so sweet and shy.' Ruby twirls a red curl and giggles. 'He'll be like my training wheels.'

My ears are burning. My lips are frozen. *Training wheels!*

'What nice times?' Tina asks. Thankfully, her lips still work.

I'm going to puke. Here come the carrots. I hate you Ruby Sivler.

'Well, it was after you moved to Maine last year Willa –'

Thanks a lot, Stella. Always messing up my life . . .

'– Joey and I were Spanish partners and had to write a skit for Cinco de Mayo –'

I'm having a sinking feeling of déjà vu. Ruby somehow managed to be JFK's Spanish partner in seventh grade too. *What is wrong with you Willa? Why didn't you switch to Spanish then? Who cares if you've had six years of French? Spanish is a perfectly good language. Half the country speaks it. How hard can it be? Maybe I can still . . .*

'– and Joey would come over to my house just about every day after school so we could work on the skit. Day after day, we'd be sitting side by side at the computer, all alone, down in the basement –' Ruby looks like she's blushing. She twirls a red curl. I'd like to rip that curl out by its roots – 'and then one afternoon Joey just leaned over and –' Ruby pauses for maximum dramatic effect.

My head is spinning, the soup is rising.

'He leaned over and what?' Tina demands.

'Oh –' Ruby tilts her head and twirls another evil curl – 'I can't say.' She's smiling, innocent as Little Red Riding Hood. 'It's sort of our secret.'

The cafeteria's crashing in on me. I turn to run. 'Willa, wait,' Tina calls. The bell rings. Ironically, I've got French.

Mademoiselle Ferret looks especially constipated today. That lady never cracks a smile. 'Pop quiz,' she announces gleefully. Pop quizzes are Ferret's idea of fun. She really ought to take up fossil-hunting or something.

'Willafred?'

I hate that. Ferret insists on using my full name. Stella used to do that too, back in the BS

– Before Sam – days. Imagine having to endure 'Willafred' when you could be 'Willa like a willow tree' instead?

'*Oui, Mademoiselle.*'

She tells me to please stand and conjugate the verb "to love".'

Love? Do ferrets have sick psychic senses or what?

I stand fighting back tears and puke.

'*J'aime.*' *I* was beginning to love JFK.

'*Tu aimes.*' *You* might not believe it, but I thought he liked me too.

'*Il ou elle aime.*' Now, I find out, *he* loves Ruby and *she* loves him.

'*Nous aimons.*' *We* could have been a great couple.

Last period is Class Meeting. We're voting on our Community Service project. I've forgotten all about the library. All I can think about is JFK.

11

'Hot, hot, hot'

The poor soul sat sighing by a sycamore tree,
Sing all a green willow:
Her hand on her bosom, her head on her knee,
Sing willow, willow, willow.

— **Shakespeare,** *Othello*

Come on Willa. Get a grip. You've got a job to do.
Think how you love that library. Just tell them the
plan and you can go home, crawl into bed and cry.

I sit with the other class officers up front. Ruby
and the Burners aren't here. Good. JFK is sitting on
the couch in the back corner with his headphones
on and his eyes closed. His lips are moving fast as
an auctioneer at Sotheby's and his curls are in sync
with the beat. Rap, he said, 'It's like poetry except
it's music.'

Our class president, Gus Groff, the smartest kid in Bramble, keeps us on schedule. We decide on important issues we want to tackle with the administration. More 'outie' days. Less homework. Important issues.

'Willa, you're on,' Gus nods to me.

When I take the podium, JFK takes his headphones off.

Be brave, Willa, be brave. I smile and he smiles back. He pulls the two-pounder out of his backpack, unwraps some candy and gives me a thumb's up sign.

Ha ha, Ruby, so there.

'Willa,' Gus taps his watch.

'Thanks, Gus.' I'm feeling more confident. 'Hi every—'

The door plunges open. Ruby and the other freshmen Burners gush in, giggling. Ruby plops down on the couch next to JFK. The other Burners sqwoosh in beside her, sandwiching Ruby closer and closer, until she's practically on JFK's lap.

My throat clenches. *Forget about her, Willa.* 'As you know, we need to decide on our community-service project. Some way in which our class can make a better a Bramble. I have a suggestion, but I'd like to hear other ideas.'

No one says anything. Just as I expected. Nobody else wanted this job. 'OK then.' This should go as smooth as taffy. 'You've probably heard about—'

'Let's get some decent vending machines,' Luke calls out.

'Yeah, that's good,' Emily says, and several girls nod.

'OK.' I write 'IDEAS' on the board and then '#1 Vending Machines'.

'And a new sound system for the gym,' Jessie says. The Buoys are on a roll.

'Nice one,' Tina says, smiling at Jessie.

Hey, Tina, you're on my team. And it will take more than a new sound system to make The Buoy Boys sound better. But Sam says that when you're brainstorming, you're just supposed to let people be creative and get all their ideas out. You write down everything everyone says without trashing it and then you go back and talk about it later. If it comes to a vote though, Tina, you'd better pick me. Ice cream or not.

'Good. Number two, sound system.' I write it on the board. 'Anybody else?'

The room is silent. 'OK, then, if no one else has any ideas, I have a sugges—'

There's a mumble from the back.

'I'm sorry,' I say. 'What was that?'

'Vanity lights,' Ruby shouts.

The Burners giggle. JFK smiles. He must think this is funny.

'What do you mean by vanity lights?' I'm breaking the brainstorming rules, but that is a stupid idea. If looks could kill, Ruby would be 'roll over, rover, you're dead'.

'Well it's no secret we need better lighting in the girls' locker room,' Ruby says like she's done extensive research on this crucial crisis.

'That's right,' the Burners say.

'So we can see ourselves better,' Ruby says, puffing up like a peacock.

'That's right,' the Burners agree.

'It's impossible to put on mascara, or curl your lashes, and you might as well forget about eyeliner –'

'That's right,' the Burners are outraged. These are horrible hardships indeed.

Ruby marches on like she's giving a campaign speech. '– and so, in conclusion –' Ruby poofs her red curls and bats her eyelashes fast as a hummingbird – 'I say better lights for a better Bramble.'

The Burners cheer, 'Hot, hot, hot.'

Ruby has got to be kidding. This will be easy. I look at JFK. He winks at me. 'And you think this is an important cause,' I say, standing up on my soapbox, the scales of truth and justice on my side. 'You want to make a better Bramble by buying new lights for the *bathroom*?'

Gus and his chess-club friends crack up. The Latin-club kids do too.

Ruby's cheeks turn as red as her hair.

'OK,' I say, turning towards the board, feeling a tiny bit bad for being so mean, but only a really tiny bit, 'fine. number three, vanity lights.'

When I turn around, Ruby's on the rebound. She sits back down on the couch, skin close as she can to JFK. 'Oh, and . . .' Ruby pauses. She turns and looks at JFK with a mischievous smile. 'I don't

want to discriminate against *boys* or anything.'
Ruby keeps staring right at JFK. She puts her
hand on his arm. Someone says, 'Ooh-ooh,' and
the Burners squeal.

'It's just that I've never been in the *boy's* locker
room before –'

The swim-team guys slap their elbows together
and bark out their seal call, *urgh, urgh, urgh* . . .

JFK looks flustered.

'– and so I'm not exactly sure how *dark it is* in
there . . .'

The Burners sing, 'Hot, hot, hot.'

The whole room is laughing. Now JFK is redder
then Ruby's hair. Is he embarrassed or guilty or
what? My head is spinning. Breathe, Willa, breathe.
I turn back to the board and pretend I'm fixing
a word that's smudged. Tears are stinging my
eyes. Is there something I don't know? Did Ruby
and JFK kiss in the locker room? Stop it, Willa.
Get a grip. Don't you dare cry. Do you hear
me?

'Willa,' Gus calls. 'There's another hand.'

I force the tears back in and turn around. It's
JFK. He's waiting for me to call on him. I nod and

turn back to the board so I don't have to see his face. I write '# 4'.

'What about you, Willa,' JFK says.

I'm so confused. What is he doing? Who does he like, Ruby or me?

'You said you had a good suggestion.'

I can't speak.

'Yeh, Willa,' Tina chimes in. 'That's right. What's your idea?'

'Willa?' Gus prompts, nodding toward the clock. 'We're out of time.'

For a few seconds, I'm frozen. But then I picture the green ivy waving on that old brick building, the whale spoutin' fountain, Mrs Saperstone all excited handing me a book . . . all those rows of beautiful books.

I take a deep breath. This is bigger than a boy.

'Well, I don't know how many of you have heard the news,' I start in a shaky voice, 'but the town council is closing the Bramble Library . . .'

Somehow I managed to finish. Nobody looks very interested. The bell rings. Kids are leaving. Gus says, 'Maybe we should table the vote.'

'Hey, wait,' Tina shouts, rushing up front to

join me. 'Willa's right, everybody. Maybe we can get on TV or something. You know, saving the poor old library. And we won't do *fund*-raisers, we'll do FUN-raisers. Fun, fun, fun.'

'Sounds good to me,' JFK says louder than I have ever heard him speak. He walks up to stand by me and Tina. 'Count me in. I vote for the library too.'

My heart is pounding. My head is spinning. A volcano is erupting inside.

'Joey's right,' Ruby says, coming up next to him. 'I vote for the library too.'

Gus calls for a vote. 'It's unanimous.' I run off gasping for air. All I want to do is go home, lock my door and collapse, but I'm one of the best strikers in our class and if we win the Faculty-Student soccer game it means no homework for the weekend.

JFK and I are both forwards in the fourth quarter.

'Willa,' he calls over to me. I can't look at him.

The ref calls 'two minutes'. We're tied with the teachers. I trap the ball and dribble down the field. JFK is shouting, 'Willa, I'm open, pass, pass.' I can't look at him. My head and my heart are colliding. I charge on and slam in that ball so hard that poor goalie, Swammy, makes a suicide dive that sends his turban sailing. Sorry, Swammy.

'Willa!' JFK shouts as I blast away on my bike. 'Willa, wait. What's wrong?'

12

'Oh, Jo-e-o, My Jo-e-o . . .'

I'll not budge an inch.

– **Shakespeare, The Taming of the Shrew**

The front door slams behind me. The Blazers look up from their Monopoly game. They are in the midst of a serious real-estate transaction, but they manage smiles as I pass. Monopoly is fun, but I'm more of a Scrabble girl.

Stella calls to join them in the kitchen. She's chopping basil and tomatoes. Sam is slicing baguettes. Garlic is crackling in the frying pan. Gorgonzola is waiting on the counter. The famous Bramblebriar bruschetta the food critics rave about. Hmm. Yum.

'The Blazers spoke with me today,' Stella says, 'about your Halloween party.'

Oh gosh, the money. 'Yes, we owe them change. I'll go find them right now.'

'They didn't say anything about change,' Stella says, still chopping, 'but they did say they had a wonderful time and they want to dance again when they come back at Thanksgiving. Sam and I were thinking we could bring in some space heaters and . . .'

While Stella talks, I keep thinking about JFK and how he kept calling to me after the game and maybe, just maybe, Ruby was making the whole Cinco de Mayo and locker thing up . . . and what should we do next to raise money for the library . . . maybe something for Thanksgiving . . . another dance in the barn . . . and JFK will come and . . .

'Willa,' Stella says. 'Are you listening to me?'

'I'll do it!' I say.

'Do what?' Stella looks confused. Sam nods patiently, it's OK, go on.

'To raise money for the library, we want to have dances and other events here at the Inn, in the barn, starting with something at Thanksgiving, then—'

Stella starts in with questions, but Sam says, 'It's nearly six o'clock, Stell.'

Way to go, Sam.

Stella looks at the clock and jumps up. 'We're late. Open the bar, Sam. I'll be right there.' Stella sprinkles Parmesan cheese on the bruschetta, quickly checks her face in the mirror, then, just when I think I'm good to go, Stella turns and says, 'I'm not agreeing to anything at this point, Willa, except a Thanksgiving dance for the Blazers.'

Tina comes over for help with math. She plops down on my bed, scattering my notebooks. 'Ruby didn't know you liked Joey.'

'What?' I'm not buying this.

'Come on, Willa. Give Ruby a break. You didn't tell her you have a crush on Joey. You never tell her anything. You don't even like her.'

'Ruby's all right.'

Tina's not buying this. 'When Stella was a wedding planner, Ruby would have cashed her trust funds for some celebrity wedding dirt, but you wouldn't dish a crumb.'

'But, Tina, what was that whole thing about the boys' locker room?'

'Oh, Willa, Ruby's a drama queen. Sort of like that freaky Lady Macbeth.'

So Tina reads her Shakespeare after all.

'Besides,' Tina says, 'I grilled Ruby like a burger about the "good times" she had with Joey doing that Spanish thing together and, you know what? I don't think they even kissed. I think Ruby's just trying to make it *seem* like they were a couple. But just to be sure, why don't I see what I can get out of Joey.'

'No, Tina.'

'Oh, Willa, come on. I haven't been watching soaps since I was six weeks old for nothing. I know how to dig without—'

'No, Tina, I mean it.'

'Come on, Willa.'

'No, no, no.'

'That's not fair, Willa. You're always talking about being fair. I know Joey's a boy, but he's a person too. Doesn't he have the right to tell his side of the story?'

Tina's good. She's very good. I sit silent for a

while. 'OK, Tina, talk to him a little, but please don't mention my name. I don't want him to think that I lo-*liiike*—'

'Love?' Tina's eyes are balloons about to pop.

'*Like*, Tina. I said like.'

'*Love*,' Tina sways to the centre of the room, swishes her hair like a veil. 'Jo-e-o . . .' She raises her chin, fists clenched to her chest, and closes her eyes. 'Oh, Jo-e-o, my Jo-e-o. How do I *love* thee, Jo-e-o? Let me count the ways—'

'Shut up, Tina,' I throw a pillow at her.

'Oh, Willa, lighten up. It happens to the best of us.'

'What about you, Tina? Have you found ten things in common with Jessie?'

'Just about,' she says, 'look.' She opens her math notebook. 'We both have the same favourite band and TV show and . . .'

After dinner, the 'Blazin'' limousine pulls up out front. A chauffer puts the Blazers' luggage into the trunk. Stella gives them a goody bag for the ride.

Mama B smothers me in hug. 'Goodbye, Willa, honey. It's been great.'

'We'll be back for the Thanksgiving Tango,' Papa B says.

'With roses in our teeth.' Mama B says. She wiggles her butt. 'Cha, cha, cha.'

'Wait,' I say. 'I've got your change from the Halloween party.'

'Oh, no, Willa,' Mama B waves her hand. 'That's for you and your friends. We'd have paid a million for that much fun, right Bell?'

Bell shakes his head. 'Absolutely, hootly. Best time we've had in years.'

The Blazers blow kisses. We wave goodbye. The chauffeur tips his hat.

I finish *The Tempest* as fast as I can so I can get to my journal. I feel better after I write. When I fall asleep though, a weird dream begins. The bad witch cackles, 'Who are you kidding, Willa my pretty? Of course JFK likes Ruby. She's beautiful and booby and a Bramble Burner . . .' Then the good witch glides in. 'Don't worry, Willa, honey. Click your cleats three times.' Then the Blazers, waving boas, rise up in a hot-air balloon, 'Bye, Willa, be back soon! Wouldn't miss the "*Thanksgiving Tango*"!'

I bolt out of bed in a sweat. *Oh no, Stella, what have you done?*

I run down the hall. The light is on. Thankfully they're still awake.

'A tango! No, Mother. My friends don't tango.'

'Well, they can have fun learning,' Stella says, smearing white cream on her face. 'I promised Chickles and Bellford. It's their favourite dance.'

'Mother, please, the party is for teenagers, not some old—'

'I thought the party was for the library?' Stella has a mummy face now.

'It is, Mother, but, come on, *the tango*?'

'The Turkey Tango,' Stella says.

'The *Turkey* Tango?'

'Yes, that's right. Chickles came up with the name and Bellford loved it and so I said that's what we'd call it.'

'Mother, how could you?'

'I'm sorry, Willa, but they are important guests. I am, we are, running a *business* here. Besides, I'm sure by now they've already told all their relatives and—'

'Oh no. Why didn't you ask me before you ruined my whole—'

'OK, ladies,' Sam says, putting down his book. 'Let's take a breather.'

Sam would have made a dandy diplomat.

'There must be a compromise.' He smiles. 'Remember . . . it takes two to tango.'

Uggh. I could spit at my mother I'm so mad.

I stare at her. She stares at me. Neither one of us will budge an inch.

13

Be a Ruffler

My library was dukedom large enough.

— **Shakespeare,** *The Tempest*

I wake up thinking about two very different things.

One, JFK. Two, the Bramble Library

JFK will have to wait. The town council meets tonight.

I change the quote on the Bramble Board.

> My library was dukedom large enough.
> — William Shakespeare

'Perfect words, Willa,' Sam says.

Finding words for the Bramble Board was easy; finding words for tonight is not. All I know for certain is that they are not going to close my library. I'll charge in like Joan of Arc, mighty sword, trusty stallion, my legion of valiant kinsmen by my side.

I try rallying my legion at school. Only Tina promises to come. JFK is off sick.

'Willa, people just aren't into this like you are,' Tina says. 'I mean, the library's nice and books are nice, but what's that got to do with us? I mean, if you want a book, go buy one. If you're doing a paper, go online. I mean, maybe libraries are becoming dinosaurs. Maybe it's just their time to go extinct or some—'

'*Dinosaurs? Extinct?* Tina, that's not even funny . . .'

But Tina is off in another zone, fixing her make-up with extreme concentration.

My speech is going to have to be good. Really, really good.

And so, while my lab partner, Jay Zonderman, is dissecting our frog in Biology, poor little slimy green thing, I'm thinking about what to say tonight.

And while Mr Kay, our Algebra teacher, is

explaining how to calculate the hidden assets of unknown integers, I'm jotting down notes for my speech.

And while Mademoiselle Ferret is delivering a monologue as if it's opening night in Paris, I'm watching like I'm absolutely mesmerized, but inside I'm imagining how I will deliver my own speech tonight. I'll start off serious and fill their heads with facts and then travel south until I'm pulling on heart-strings. *Plunk. Plunk. Plunk.*

The only problem is, I haven't figured out the heart-strings part, and that is the really important part. How do I reach the council members' hearts? What makes them tick? I don't even know these horrible people. But I know who does.

After school I race to the library. Thankfully, it's open.

'Come on in, Willa,' Mrs Saperstone says. 'Let's see what we can do.'

It's cold in here. Mrs Saperstone is wearing gloves. She sits at her desk by the window. I plop down in a chair. We look out at the big grey whale.

I keep my mouth closed. Stella says sometimes I talk so much, people can't hear themselves think. So I sit back and 'zip the lips' as my fourth-grade music teacher used to say. Actually, music class would have been a whole lot nicer if Miss Bisket had zipped *her* lips. That woman could rip the fun out of any song. She could just rip out the fun the way they yanked out rotten teeth in Shakespeare's time.

Mrs Saperstone is staring out the window, so quiet and patient. It's amazing we are kindred spirits. I'm quiet sometimes, yes, but no way am I patient. I was born without the patience gene. I got triple worries, zero patience.

After a few minutes that feel like an hour, Mrs Saperstone looks at me.

'We've got to make it *personal*,' she says.

'That's right,' I say. 'We've got to tug at their hearts somehow.'

Mrs Saperstone nods, then she's off to her thinking again.

I get up and walk around. This place brings back so many memories. I stop at the L-M aisle. The *Frog and Toad* books by Arnold Lobel. Mrs

Saperstone introduced me to them one summer long ago. I read them over and over again. Frog and Toad were best friends. I wanted one of those, a best friend. A frog or a toad, it didn't matter. But with all the moving we'd done my books had to be my best friends.

'Sign this, will you, Willa?'

I walk back to the window.

Mrs Saperstone looks excited. 'The pen is mightier than the sword,' she says.

Mrs Saperstone hands me a pen and an index card. It says, Bradbury, Ray, *Fahrenheit 451*, and under that, 'Date' and 'Borrower's Name' with rows of blue lines.

'What is this?' I ask.

'It's the old-fashioned way we used to borrow books in Bramble. You signed your name on the card in the pocket in the back. Signing your name made it personal. Like you were borrowing something special.'

'Nice,' I say, not quite sure what this has to do with my speech.

Mrs Saperstone nods. 'One of the nicest parts was that you could look at the card and see who had read that book before you. When you read the names, you felt a connection to those people. And when you signed your name, you connected yourself to all the people who would read that book after you.'

I nod my head. I understand.

'A book is a living thing, Willa. It soaks into your mind and heart and shapes how you think and feel. Every book you read becomes a part of you.'

Mrs Saperstone walks to a case and runs her hands over the spines. She turns to me and laughs, a far away look on her face.

'Sometimes, Willa, I'll see a smudge of sauce on a page where there's a funny scene and I think maybe the person who read this book before me was eating pizza when she laughed at this part. Or I'll see a tear-size stain on a sad page and I'll wonder about the person who read this passage and was moved to cry just like me . . .'

When Mrs Saperstone finishes, I am excited. 'You've got to tell this to the council tonight, Mrs Saperstone.'

'No, Willa, they've heard me so often, they

don't listen any more. This old library needs a new champion.'

I look at *Fahrenheit 451*. 'Why did you pick this for me?' I ask.

'Read it and you'll understand. It's one of those books you never forget.'

I start signing my name and as I do I get a crazy idea. 'You know the council members, right, Mrs Saperstone?'

'Of course, I know them well.'

'And did they sign out books from this library when they were kids?'

'Well, not the wash-ashores like Harry Sivler, but Phinny Langerhorn surely did, and Phoebe Slingerlands, and of course Josiah Bulmer's father's the one who donated the whale fountain because he was such a fan of *Moby*—'

'That's it!' I nearly knock her down with a hug. I tell her my plan.

'Oh no, Willa. I can't.'

'Yes you can, Mrs Saperstone. Yes you can.'

Finally, Mrs Saperstone agrees. She makes a list of the seven people on the Bramble Town Council and then says, 'OK, let's go.'

I put *451* in my backpack and follow Mrs Saperstone upstairs, past the Reading Room, where JFK was writing that day. She opens a door at the end of the hall and pulls a string to turn on the light. There are rows of dusty filing cabinets with dates on the front of each. Mrs Saperstone locates a certain cabinet, unlocks it and begins shuffling through the files. She closes one and moves to another cabinet, making notes.

'This is bravest thing I've ever done,' Mrs Saperstone says.

Wow. Zip the lips, Willa. Zip the lips.

'I could lose my job over this.' She lets out a laugh. 'But then, I probably will anyway. I might as well have some fun. You know, Willa, since I was a little girl, I've done what is expected me. I've followed the rules. I've toed the line. I've never ruffled any feathers. Today, I'm going to be a ruffler.'

14

In the Pocket

All the world's a stage,
And all the men and women merely players:
They have their exits and their entrances;
And one man in his time plays many parts.

– Shakespeare, *As You Like It*

The first person I recognize when we enter Town Hall, Meeting Room A, is Ruby Sivler's father. He's sitting with the other council members at the long table at the head of the room. He says something and the man next to him laughs.

'Speak loudly and clearly,' Stella says, coaching me, 'and make eye contact with the decision makers.' Stella is happy to share the wisdom of her MBA. 'And if you start shaking or sweating, just keep smiling confidently and no one will notice.'

Oh, great. I know Stella's intentions are good, but she's making me even more nervous. The spaghetti from dinner is swirling in my stomach.

Sam walks me to the check-in area and I sign my name under the 'Public Comments' heading. I tell him about my stomach.

Sam puts his hand on my shoulder. 'Butterflies are good, Willa. Actors hope for butterflies before they go on stage. It means they care about the part. Otherwise the performance falls flat.'

Nana and Gramp come in wearing sneakers. Good, Nana walked. Next comes Tina, Sulamina Mum and Swammy. Mrs Saperstone said it was my turn tonight.

The meeting drags on for hours. Finally, 'Open comment on the library issue.' I walk to the front of the room. A few council members smile, others are talking, or writing, not paying attention to me. I read the names on the placards.

First in the row is the Chairman, Phinneus T. Langerhorn III. He's wearing a fancy pinstriped suit and yellow bow tie. I check my list and reach in my bag. When I hand him the old book, he looks confused.

'It's *Treasure Island*,' I say.

Phinneus T. Langerhorn III opens the frayed jacket. He leafs slowly through the pages, pausing to look at an illustration. He slaps the book shut. 'That's nice.'

'Look in the back,' I say. 'In the pocket.'

Mr Langerhorn III opens the back cover. He takes out the card. 'I haven't seen one of these in years.' A wave of emotion flickers across his wrinkled face. 'Hmmph,' he sniffs, clearing his throat. 'Look at this.' He points out something to Mr Sivler. 'That was me, Phinny Langerhorn, a long time ago.'

The next one on the list is Miss Phoebe Slingerlands, the richest and most powerful woman in Bramble. She was a famous botanist, even discovered some new species of royal lilies. Right now she looks royally bored.

I reach in my bag and find the right book. 'Miss Slingerlands.'

'*Little Women*,' she says. 'How sweet.' She hands it back to me.

'Look in the pocket,' I say, giving the book back to her.

Miss Slingerlands pulls out the card. She adjusts her glasses and begins reading the names aloud: 'Devon Bender, Faith Picotte, Peggy McGarry, oh, my good friend, Peg . . . oh, and look, there I am, Phoebe Slingerlands.' Miss Slingerlands's lips tremble. She closes the book.

'Look on page twenty-one,' I whisper.

Earlier, when we went through the books Mrs Saperstone and I had found, classics that certain members of this Board had read as children, I noticed that in *Little Women,* a book Miss Slingerlands had renewed three times as a girl, there was a notation on page twenty-one. Next to a passage about Beth March, the girl in the book who loved to play piano, someone had written 'me too' and signed the initials 'P.S.'.

Miss Slingerlands opens to page twenty-one. 'Oh,' she gasps, bringing her fingers to her lips. 'I forgot how I loved that piano.'

Josiah Bulmer is ready for me. 'I know. *Moby Dick*, right?'

'Just call me Ishmael,' I say, handing him the famous whale tale.

And so it went on, through *Great Expectations* and *Tom Sawyer* . . .

After I handed out the last book, I circulated copies of my research on the importance of libraries. I guess it made sense to do the heart stuff before the head stuff, because now the council members were paying attention, even encouraging me.

But in the end, it was all about the money.

'Thank you for coming, Miss Havisham. It was a fine presentation,' Mr Langerhorn III says. Several board members nod their heads in agreement.

'Yes, good job, Willa,' Mr Sivler says, 'I'd hire you. But the bottom line is, the bank is foreclosing. We have several competing concerns and limited resources. Roadway maintenance, beach access issues . . . we all feel badly about the library, but something's got to give. The funds just aren't there.'

'How much money do we need?' I ask.

'More than we can squeeze out of this budget,' Mr Sivler says, motioning like I'm dismissed.

'Well, how much?' I ask again. 'The Bramble Academy freshman class will be holding fundraising events all year long and every penny we raise will go towards saving the Bramble Library . . .' There's a ripple of laughter and people talking. Miss Slingerlands peers out at me over her glasses as if suddenly I'm a more interesting specimen. Sulamina Mum clears her throat loudly, *Hghmm*, like be quiet and listen to my girl. Swammy straightens his shoulders and makes that 'settle down' look he does in Shakespeare. Sam nods his head. Stella is smiling. Tina gives me a thumb's up.

Phinneus T. Langerhorn III adjusts his yellow bow tie. 'That's very nice, Miss Havisham. Please tell your classmates how grateful the Board is for your civic-mindedness. Truly, it is impressive. But the debt is just too great at this point.'

'But exactly how much do we need?' I ask, holding my ground.

'Too much,' Mr Sivler snaps. He doesn't think this is funny.

'I'm sorry, young lady,' Mr Langerhorn says. 'But it's really already been decided. We've made an excellent arrangement with the town of Falmouth to consolidate the collections and—'

'But this is the town of *Bramble*,' I say. 'And these are *Bramble* books.'

Nana and Gramp start clapping and the rest of my cheering section joins in.

'That's true,' Mr Langerhorn's face flushes red. 'But the bank is fore—'

'*OK*,' Tina says in a loud voice. She struts up to the podium next to me.

'OK,' Tina says again. 'This is the *third time* my friend has asked you people, *how much money do we need?*'

'Fifty thousand dollars,' Mr Sivler shouts.

'OK,' I say. 'Now we're getting somewhere.'

15

Dancing for Dickens

What's in a name? That which we call a rose
By any other name would smell as sweet.

— Shakespeare, *Romeo and Juliet*

'You and Tina make quite a tag team,' Sam says to us at Mama Java's Cafe. Stella had to hurry home, but Sam said we should celebrate. Tina ordered a double mocha cherry fusion carmellata cappuccino, grande. Sam and I got hot chocolate.

'The scene was perfectly executed,' Dr Swammy agrees, sipping his ginger tea. 'Bravo, ladies. I expect you both to try out for the spring play.'

'Willa wasn't acting tonight,' Sulamina Mum says. 'That was straight from the heart.' She pats her fist against her hefty chest. 'Good job, little sister.'

'We're proud of you, honey,' Nana says. 'And you too, Tina.'

Gramp Tweed nods. 'Couldn't be prouder.'

Tonight was a huge success. I can't wait to tell Mrs Saperstone. Mr Sivler kept objecting, but Phoebe Slingerlands said, 'Give them till winter's end' and the council agreed not to make a final decision until the fifteenth February. If we raise $10,000 by then, they will petition the bank to extend the mortgage on the remaining $40,000.

Now all we have to do is raise $10,000. Ten *thousand* dollars.

Tina and I start writing ideas for fundraising events on a napkin.

'Did you know the Beatles wrote some of their best lyrics on napkins?' I ask.

'No, Willa, I didn't. That's fascinating.'

'OK,' I say, 'November.' When I tell Tina about the Turkey Tango I think she'll flip, but she says, 'Are we stuck with the name?'

'Yep.'

'OK, no problem. We'll find a way to make it fun. Now, December . . . let's have a prom. We can call it the Snow Ball.'

'But doesn't it take months to plan a prom?'

'You're right,' Tina says sadly.

'How about a winter carnival?' I suggest. 'We could still call it the Snow Ball. We've got cross-country trails behind the Inn and Sam's making an even bigger ice-skating rink this year. And maybe we could do a snowman-making contest . . .'

Mum's on board. Tina's miles away. 'How does that sound, Tina?'

'Cold, Willa. It sounds cold. We've got to think *fun*. Wait . . . I know!' Her face brightens. 'How about a summer beach party? We can dump sand on the floor, hire a DJ, gets some grills going with hotdogs and burgers, wear our *bathing suits*!'

I write down December Beach Party. 'I still like the snowman idea.' I'd rather wear a snow-suit than a bathing suit next to Tina and Ruby.

'Sure, well, maybe we can do that too,' Tina says without conviction.

'Now, January,' I say. 'How about a Rock 'n' Roll Bowl-for-Books night?'

'Sounds like fun,' Mum says, taking a sip of her coffee.

Tina crinkles her nose. 'Bor-ing. We can do better.'

'What's wrong with bowling, Tina? I like—'

'We've got to think *boys* here, Willa, *boys*. In January every boy in Bramble will be thinking Super Bowl. The Pats have a shot this year.'

'OK,' I say. 'February's easy: Valentine's Day. How about a fancy dance?'

'Now you're talking, Willa. We know who you'll be slow-smooching with.'

'*Shhhh,*' I say. Mum winks at me.

'At least by then you'll know if you're *compatible* or not,' Tina keeps it up.

Thankfully Sam and Swammy are discussing school. Nana and Gramp are talking to the Reillys at the next table about their trip to New York City.

'It's not all about compatibility,' I tell Tina in a low voice.

'Oh, that's right,' she says. 'I forgot about the flying baby.'

Mum laughs. I roll my eyes. But what if Tina's right? What if JFK and I have nothing in common but cider doughnuts? I like soccer. He likes football . . .

'Wait,' Tina says, her eyes lighting up like sparklers. 'Let's test it out.'

'Test what out?' I'm confused. By the look on Mum's face, she is too.

'Let's see which works better, compatibility or Cupid.'

'How?' I'm not sure I want to hear the answer.

'Well, you know I've been working on ten questions like my Aunt Amber's "Perfect Ten." How about if everyone who buys a ticket for the dance has to answer "Tina's Ten?" I'll get Aunt Amber to match up the most-compatible couples and they'll have to dance a special slow song together. Afterwards, we'll see if the matches stick. If they do, compatibilty rules. If not . . . well, maybe Cupid's cool.'

'Sounds fun,' Mum says with a laugh. We both look at her.

'Oh, sorry, girls.' Mum stops smiling.

'Hey, Mum,' I ask. 'Did you ever write that letter?'

'Well, yes. I took your advice, Willa, about being a leaper. I called our old school and got an address and wrote to Riley, but I guess he decided not to—'

'What are you talking about?' Tina interrupts.

'Nothing, honey,' Mum says. 'It's getting late. Thanks for the coffee, Sam.'

After Mum leaves, I tell Tina the story.

'Really?' Tina says. 'Mum had a boyfriend! Wow . . . OK, enough about that. What should we name the February dance?'

'Let's see,' I say, shifting gears. 'It's for the library. Maybe something about books?' I think for a minute . . . 'How about "Dancing for Dickens?"'

Tina looks disgusted. 'That's a horrible name. We need something romantic. Something about the perfect matches we're going to make—'

'Don't forget Cupid.'

'Cupid's stupid, Willa, this is serious.'

'Well,' I say, 'if you don't like Dickens. What about Shakespeare? How about *A Midwinter Night's Dream*? Remember how we read *A Mid*summer—'

'I love it,' Tina says. '*A Midwinter Night's Dream* it is.'

'We still need to run all of this by the Community Service Committee,' I say.

'Whatever,' Tina says. She's writing on a napkin. I look over her shoulder.

What's your favourite pizza topping? What's your favourite Cape beach . . .

Later when we drop Tina off, she says, 'Don't forget tomorrow's a dud.' That's what we call a 'dress uniform day'. Blazers and dress shoes required. 'See ya, dud.'

After I get the whole happy story of my speech to the council in my journal, I raid the kitchen for leftovers. When I come back upstairs, I hear Stella talking.

'Fifty thousand dollars? Sounds fishy to me, Sam. There's something else going on here. I bet Harry Sivler's up to something . . .'

I want to eavesdrop, but I don't. I want to keep the good feeling of what I accomplished tonight. Just wait until Mrs Saperstone hears!

I unwrap a lime taffy, pop it in, and open *Fahrenheit 451*. Big mistake. It sucks me in. I can't put it down. The wrappers pile up as I read.

Matchmaker Saperstone strikes again.

16

Rain into Rainbows

How far that little candle throws his beams!
So shines a good deed in a naughty world.

– Shakespeare, *The Merchant of Venice*

Sam and Stella and I are in our usual seats at BUC. Nana and Gramp too. Sunlight is streaming through the prisms hanging in the tall-paned windows, making tiny rainbows everywhere. Rainbows dancing on the walls, dancing on people's faces.

Mum enters in her crazy-coloured robe, turns toward a window, arms stretched wide, smiling like, as Mum would say, she 'just saw Jesus'. And then she sings 'Here Comes the Sun'.

Mum faces us. 'Good morning, sisters and brothers. Happy new day to you. Tomorrow, the thirteenth of November, is World Kindness Day. Time to turn rain into rainbows.'

Mum passes out boxes of pencils and pieces of paper cut out in the shape of a hand. It's a big hand. Mum must have traced her own.

'I want you to write down one kind thing you are going to do for another person this week. And I mean *do*, sisters and brothers, *do*. Not just think about, or talk about, or offer to, or promise to, but one kind thing you are going to DO for someone.'

I put my hand on top of Mum's hand. Mine is so much smaller.

'And if the *someone* is a someone you've had troubles with, that's even better. Turn that rain into rainbows, my friends. Rain into rainbows, it's all in your hands.'

I sneak a side peek at Stella. I wonder what she's thinking about.

At the end of the service, Mum gets us all up singing and clapping together:

'We've got the whole world in our hands.
We've got the whole wide world in our hands.

We've got the whole world in our hands.
We've got the whole world in our hands . . .'

Ruby Sivler and her parents are in front of us. Mrs Sivler is swaying her black miniskirted hips like she's at a rock concert. Mr Sivler is stiff as a goalpost. Ruby turns around and gives me her paper hand. It says, 'Beauty consult, your place or mine?'

I am Ruby's act of kindness.

At first I'm insulted, but then I remember how I wanted to ask Ruby for her opinion on my hair anyway. I lean forward and whisper, 'How about your house?'

'Great,' she whispers back. 'Tomorrow after school.'

After bagels, I walk to Sweet Bramble Books with Nana and Gramp. Nana wants me to try out three new Thanksgiving taffy flavours.

'My scouts tell me Ghelfi's is going all out,' Nana says. Cabot's in Ptown has a lock-hold on the Outer Cape, but around here, Ghelfi's and Nana are arch rivals.

'I think I won Halloween,' Nana says, 'but Thanksgiving is anybody's turkey.'

The first piece of taffy is an ugly greyish-brown. It tastes ugly too. The next one tastes like ginger snaps. Nice. The third is delicious. It tastes like a Heath bar.

'I'd drop the first one, Nana.'

'The "No Bluffin' Stuffin"?'

'Yep. You're going to make people puke.'

'How about the "Ginger-Gravy, Baby"?'

'That's a keeper,' I say.

'And what about the "Talkin' Turkey Toffee Taffy"?'

'Definitely. That's the best. But you should put little flavour descriptions underneath the names so people will know what to expect.'

'Good idea,' Nana says. 'You've got good candy genes, Willa. Maybe you'll take over the business some day. Clearly your mother has no interest.'

Stella's not a big candy fan.

'Gramp thinks we should have a contest for "Talkin' Turkey," Nana says. 'Any customer who can say "Talkin' Turkey Toffee Taffy" five times, fast, without flubbing up gets a five pound chocolate turkey, solid.'

I look at the clock. 'OK, here goes.

Talkin' turkey toffee taffy, talkin' tookey tofer toofy . . .'

Don't laugh. You try it. It's harder than you think.

'You're walking every day, right, Nana?'

'Yes,' she says. 'Every day. This old bat's finally hitting the Big Apple.'

'That's great, Nana.'

'We might even get on TV. Just you wait. Some December morning you'll be sitting there having your cold cereal, watching the news before school, while Stella's rushing around barking orders instead of making you the good hot breakfast you deserve, and that nice man will be doing the weather report and then all of a sudden you'll see me and Gramp with a poster waving, 'Hi, Willa! Hi, Willa!'

'You're a hoot, Nana.'

'Here, give these to Stella,' Nana says. She gives me a box of chocolate-covered mints. 'They're still her favourites, right?'

'Yep.' Stella never comes to Nana's store. She hardly ever eats sweets. Stella is a health fanatic. Runs five miles every morning. Eats organic everything. Ten tiny chocolate-covered mints is a 'splurge'. She actually counts them out.

'If you have some time, Willa, maybe you could stay and help Gramp for a bit. I'm heading up for a nap.'

I was planning to meet Tina to work on the Turkey Tango, but I say, 'Sure.'

'Is Nana OK?' I ask Gramp when she leaves. I'm worried about Nana's heart.

'Oh, she's fine, honey. A nap is one of the great gifts of old age. You don't feel guilty any more. When Nana comes down, I'm heading up for a snooze myself.'

I help Gramp stock the shelves and wait on customers. When things slow down, he makes lemon tea. We sit on the couch, feet on the ottoman and 'book talk'. We've talked so many good ones over the years . . . *The Giver, Roll of Thunder, A Day No Pigs Would Die* . . . great stories, great characters, great ideas, that made me want to read more.

'Are you enjoying Shakespeare?' Gramp asks.

'Absolutely.'

'Good. I'm glad. Here's a little something for

you, Willa. An early Christmas present.' Gramp
hands me a small wooden plaque tied with a bow.
I take off the bow and read the inscription:

> *'Who is it that says most, which can say more*
> *Than this rich praise, that you alone are you –'*
> *– William Shakespeare,* Sonnet 84

'I thought you might like to put it over your desk
or something.'

'It's beautiful, Gramp, thanks. Now what can I
get you this year?'

'Not a thing you can buy me, Willa. Just
knowing *you* is the gift.'

I give Gramp a hug. I always feel so happy
here. I tell Gramp I'm reading *Fahrenheit 451*. It's
a fantasy where the government is so threatened
by books, they order firemen to burn them.
Firefighter Guy Montag loves to watch 'while the
flapping pigeon-winged books died . . .'

'Yes,' Gramp nods, 'an important book indeed.
And not so fantastical. There will always be those
who try to keep certain books off the shelves. We
must fight that, Willa.' Gramp's voice rises. 'Writers

must be free to write the truest books they can. If you don't like a book, you can close it. But you have no right to say I can't open it.'

'That's right, Gramp.' I love this old man. I hug him. Then I try to 'lighten things up', as Tina would say. I tell Gramp about The Blazers and the upcoming Turkey Tango and how Stella hired a woman dance instructor named Shirley Happyfeet Hall from North Truro to give dance lessons. 'And I swear that's her real name, Gramp, "Happyfeet", and I'm not stretching the taffy.'

Gramp laughs so hard he wipes tears from his eyes. 'Oh ,Willa, I just love how you tell a story. I hope you're writing these things down.'

'Don't worry, Gramp. I am. You couldn't make this stuff up.'

Stella's in the kitchen, doing paperwork. 'Want some coffee?' I ask.

'Sure, thanks, that'd be nice. I've got to get these orders out.'

While the coffee's brewing I warm up some of Sam's famous banana bread.

'Is there something I can help you with, Mother?'

'No, I'm all set.' Stella sips the coffee, but pushes the banana bread away.

'Are you sure?' I say.

'Willa, please,' she sighs. 'I've got to finish this.'

I guess the kindest thing I can do for Stella is leave her alone.

I bike to the beach. The wind whooshes in my ears. I close my eyes. *Please let JFK come to the Turkey Tango and please let Ruby Sivler get strep throat that night, no . . . I know, sorry . . .*

I spot a piece of beach glass, green, and then a blue one too. Lucky duck. I stick them in my pocket for my rainbow jar at home.

17

'The Willa'

Kindness in women,
not their beauteous looks,
shall win my love.

– Shakespeare, *The Taming of the Shrew*

Community Service meets last period. Just the girls show up. 'OK,' I say, 'we can do this. If we have one fundraiser a month in November, December and January and we charge twenty dollars a ticket and fifty people come to each . . .'

'That's ten thousand dollars right there,' Tina says.

'No, that's one thousand for each event,' I say. 'And one thousand dollars times three will be three thousand dollars. Then, if we do a big formal dance in early February – maybe we can hold it in the gym – and if we get a hundred people at seventy dollars per ticket, we'll make seven thousand dollars.'

'And three thousand plus seven thousand equals ten thousand,' Tina says.

I just look at Tina. 'And then we'll make our goal by the fifteenth of February and keep the library from being closed.'

Kelsey says seventy dollars sounds like too much to charge for a dance.

'Well, just think about what you'd spend on a typical Saturday night,' Tina says. 'Movie tickets, the arcades, a super-size soda, popcorn, a box of Starburst . . .'

Nana would cringe to hear about candy from a box.

Everyone loves the name Midwinter Night's Dream.

'How about if I chair the Dream?' Ruby offers. 'I have the most experience with large-scale events,' she says. 'We need to book a venue, hire a DJ, think about decorations, start calling on local businesses for contributions . . .'

Tina looks at me like it's a good idea. I think

about Mum's act of kindness and how Ruby's going to do my hair. 'OK, Ruby. That would be great.'

Tina shares her idea about a beach party in the barn for December and I talk about a possible Super Bowl Bowling Party at Strikers in January.

I let Tina break the news about the Turkey Tango.

'Wait till you hear this,' Tina says all excited. 'You know how Thanksgiving is like the most boring holiday of the year? Stuff like a pig and watch football? Well, you know that TV show, *Star Dance*? They may come to film us dancing in Willa's barn!'

'Awesome!' Lauren says. 'I love that show. What should we wear?'

'Tina,' I whisper. 'What are you talking about?'

'I'll send them an email, Willa,' Tina whispers. 'Anything's possible, right?'

Ruby meets me at my locker after school. 'Ready?' she says, zipping her red leather jacket. 'Yep,' I say, buttoning my navy wool coat.

'We're going to have big trouble getting boys to

that Turkey Tango,' Ruby says as we walk to her house. 'We'll have to think of a lure.'

Please don't come. Get strep throat. Throw another bonfire on the beach or something. Please stay away from JFK. Just find me a good hairstyle.

Ruby's house looks like a Las Vegas hotel.

'Hi, girls,' Mrs Sivler calls from the kitchen. She's standing at a marble counter under a crystal chandelier wearing a skimpy red blouse and dangly earrings, frosting cupcakes as she watches a show on a wall-size screen.

'What kind are you making today?' Ruby asks, swiping a taste from the bowl.

A woman on the screen sobs, 'No, Kent, no.' She wrenches herself away from the hunky officer. 'I can't go on. It's over. We can't do this to Marlena any more . . .'

Mrs Sivler is riveted, spatula suspended in mid-air. 'What?' she asks Ruby.

'Nothing.' Ruby microwaves a bag of popcorn and dumps it in a bowl. 'Come on, Willa, I've got soda in my room.'

I follow Ruby up the winding staircase, sliding my hand up the brass, or is it gold, banister as we go. At the top, Ruby motions to the left 'that's the way to my parents' suite'. She turns right and I follow her like a trusty dog down the long hallway, peaking into rooms as we pass. Finally, Ruby says, 'Here we go.'

Ruby's room is red. Very, very red. The walls, the carpet, even the ceiling. And standing like an island in the centre of the Red Sea, is Ruby's bed. Seven sisters could sleep in it and never bump elbows. The bed towers so high off the ground, you actually do need to climb the wooden stairs next to it to reach the mattress. There's a billowy lace canopy with a jewel-studded crown on top. A wooden plaque on the wall reads, 'Bow or curtsy, take your pick, you are in the presence of a princess.' There's a row of fancy dolls on the window ledge and a large Patriots poster with signatures on it.

Oh great, Ruby likes the Pats. Just like JFK. I wonder how the team is doing?

Ruby swings her backpack on to the fake polar-bear rug, at least I hope it's fake, and points to the refrigerator. 'Help yourself,' she says, 'I've got everything.'

I open the fridge. She's not kidding. I take out a root beer.

Ruby goes into her dressing room and comes out wearing a Go Pats! sweatshirt.

Oh, great, Ruby *really* likes the Pats. She sees me looking at her sweatshirt. 'Hey,' Ruby says. 'I've got an idea how we can get more boys at the Turkey dance. I'll get Daddy to donate two of our box seats for a Pats game and we'll raffle them off as a prize. That'll get the guys there.'

Oh great, with my luck, JFK will win. I can picture it now. Ruby and JFK, in matching Patriot sweatshirts, waving pennants, cuddled together like polar bears . . .

'What's your sign, Willa?'

'My what?'

'Your sign. Your zodiac sign. When were you born?'

'January,' I say, a bit nervous about where this is heading, 'the thirteenth.'

'OK, Capricorn,' Ruby says. She leafs through a magazine on her nightstand. 'Interesting . . . You are entering a phase of rapid growth . . .'

I stick out my chest. I still feel like a second-grader next to Ruby and Tina.

'. . . and the grounded, rule-driven side of you will feel the need for continued structure as the new, more confident side of you experiments . . .'

Ruby puts the magazine down. 'OK, sit,' she says. 'I've got an idea.'

Ruby's dressing table is the kind movie stars have. Big bright bulbs all around. Vanity lights. 'OK,' Ruby talks to me in the mirror, fussing with my hair. 'You need something that expresses your changing personality. See me? I went red because it matches my more passionate nature. My interest in more serious romance . . .'

I swallow. My heart is pounding. What if JFK is the more serious romance?

Ruby is staring as if she read my mind. 'Don't worry, Willa. I'm going out with Chris Ruggiero, Saturday night. Have you seen him in his soccer uniform? Oh my God is he hot. I'm talking hotter than—'

'Ice cream?' I toss Ruby a crumb.

'What?' Ruby says. 'What do you mean *ice cream*?'

I tell Ruby about Tina's invention.

'Oh, that's great,' Ruby says. 'I'm going to start using that myself. Ice cream.'

'I don't think you can,' I say. 'Tina said she was getting a patent on it.'

Ruby and I laugh, just like two friends gossiping about another. I decide to throw out a really big crumb. 'Well, if you can keep a secret,' I say. 'JFK came to the Halloween Party and we ended up talking all night.'

'Oh, really?' Ruby says. 'Good for you.'

I can't tell if she's serious or not. 'Ruby, please don't say any—'

'Don't worry. My lips are sealed. Now, what to do with your hair?'

Ruby stares at me in the mirror. 'According to your horoscope, you are sort of at a dividing line between the old mousy . . . I mean the old Willa and the new Willa.'

Ruby parts my hair down the middle. She dries one side down straight with a paddle brush. 'Now for the other side.' She squeezes some 'Come and Get Me Curls!' styling gel on to her hands and slathers it on the other side of my head. She sticks a plastic thing on the blow-dryer – 'It's a diffuser,' Ruby says – and begins scrunching handfuls of my hair like she's crunching paper as she dries.

When Ruby's finished, I am two Willas. Left side curly. Right side straight.

I'm amazed. I like it. I really, really like it.

'Perfect,' Ruby nods her head. 'That's you, Willa. It looks great.'

'Thanks, Ruby.' I smile. 'I like it. What do you call this anyway?'

'I don't know,' Ruby says. 'How about "the Willa?" Hey, maybe I should get a patent on it or something.' We both laugh.

Ruby Sivler made a rainbow today.

I change the Bramble Board when I get home. It's a line from Aesop's fable 'The Lion and the Mouse': *'No act of kindness, no matter how small, is ever wasted.'*

18

The Turkey Tango

Love looks not with the eyes, but with the mind;
And therefore is wing'd Cupid painted blind.

— **Shakespeare, *A Midsummer Night's Dream***

If you've ever seen grown-ups who haven't danced in years all of a sudden start kicking it up good at a wedding or bat mitzvah or some other fancy shindig, hold that scene in your head. Now imagine the party is at your house and all your friends are there and when the grown-ups who haven't danced in years start kicking it up good, your friends turn and look at you like, *puke*, why did you ever invite me?

OK, now you're getting a glimpse of the Turkey Tango.

There was such unsightly shaking and twirling

and smooching and swirling that the barn cats fled screeching into the cold with the barn bats flapping behind, *wait, wait*!

Maybe the tango isn't the worst dance ever invented. Maybe it would be nice to watch two sexy, sultry Spanish lovers, bodies clasped tighter than two pages in a smutty novel, passionately slither across a stage in perfect rhythm to the pounding sound, but I can't even begin to paint you a pretty picture of Mama and Papa B going belly to belly, bosom to bosom, chipmunk cheek to chipmunk cheek across the barn floor with red roses dangling from their mouths.

No, you'll just have to paint that picture for yourself.

And do you think Miss 'Happyfeet' Hall from North Truro, the dance instructor Stella hired for the evening, stopped with tango tutoring?

No, Miss Happyfeet Hall did not. Miss Happyfeet Hall saw the gushing enthusiasm of the grown-ups: the Blazers brought tons of relatives with them: half our evening's admission goal, thank you very much. But, alas, Suzanna Jubilee will be delayed. She passed through the quarters with flying colours and now she's on to the Miss Daisydew semis in Orlando. Oh no, Miss Happyfeet did not stop at the tango. Happyfeet didn't earn that name for nothing. Miss Happyfeet could tell she had this crowd in the arch of her foot, and so, as the night beat on, she danced on to the polka and the foxtrot, disco, waltzes, merengues, cha-chas . . .

Who knew there were so many different dances? Scottish steps and Irish jigs, square dances, line dances, contras and cloggings, swings and salsas, twists and tarantellas, on and on and on . . .

Using Sam as a partner for 'demonstration purposes', which made Stella jealous, so was actually fun to see, Miss Happyfeet had those grown-ups slipping and sliding and sweating all night.

'Come join us, Willa!' Mum keeps shouting, queen of the conga line. *Dunta, dunta, dun, TA!* . . . *dunta, dunta, dun, TA!* And Nana and Gramp are Ginger Rogers and Fred Astaire. But Papa B Pilgrim and Mama B Pocahontas – she in full headdress, deerskin moccasins and native boa – are the hands-down, or should I say feet-down, amazin'-blazin' belles of the ball.

'This is a disaster,' Tina says, 'a *disaster*.'

'And where's the film crew from *Star Dance*?' Emily demands to know.

The boys keep trying to bolt. We have to physically drag them back in, shouting 'Free food! Pats box seats!' before they run off like the barn cats.

We're all huddled here in a horse stall, miserably watching the 'happy feet'.

JFK comes up next to me and my heart jumps. 'I like your new hair,' he says.

'Thanks.' I can't think what to say next.

'Hello, Willa, honey!' Mama B waves. She and Papa are doing freestyle.

'Oh my God,' Ruby says. 'Get a load of them.'

This is all Stella's fault.

'Come on, girls and boys,' Happyfeet calls, 'plenty of room for everyone!'

'This rots,' Jessie says.

'Let's got out of here,' Luke says.

'The *games*, Willa,' Tina pleads. 'What about the *games*?'

'OK, everybody. It's called Pin the Tush on the Turkey.' I point to the sorry pin-up bird I got at the dollar store. 'We'll cover your eyes and you take a feather and walk six steps forward. The one who pins a feather closest to the turkey's tush wins.'

Tina looks like she's going to kill me.

'Tush?' Jessie says.

'Butt,' Tina explains. 'The turkey's butt.'

'Come on, Luke, let's go.' Jessie zips his jacket.

'I've got a better idea,' Ruby says. 'Let's play kiss and guess.'

'Now we're talking,' Gus Groff says.

'How do you play?' Trish asks.

'Who cares,' Allie says. 'Anything's better than this.'

'It's *fun*,' Ruby promises. 'I learned it at Camp Okanowa. Everybody sits in a big circle, sort of like "duck, duck, goose". The "Mole" sits in the middle, blindfolded. The "Ruler" points to someone in the circle and that person has to kiss the Mole. If the Mole guesses who the "Kisser" is, the Mole wins and gets to be the Ruler.'

The swim-team guys do their seal slap, *urgh, urgh*. The Burners go, 'Hot, hot, hot.' Tina puts on lipstick. The Buoy Boys are first to sit.

'And don't worry, girls,' Ruby says. 'I brought goggles for us to wear under the blindfold so we won't mess up our mascara.'

I look at JFK. He rolls his eyes like, 'This is stupid.'

I scrunch my nose like, 'I know.'

'OK, who's the first Mole?' Ruby says. No one wants to go first.

'Come on,' Ruby says. 'What a bunch of turkeys.'

'I'll go,' JFK says, always the good sport.

JFK sits in the middle. Ruler Ruby wraps a blindfold around his eyes. She looks around the circle, then points to Tina. Tina looks at me, like, I'm sorry. I shrug my shoulders. Tina kisses JFK quick on the cheek and then hurries back to her seat.

JFK laughs. 'That was too quick. I didn't even have time to smell perfume.'

'OK,' Ruler Ruby says, 'you've got to count to five, kissers, one-thousand-one, one-thousand-two . . . We'll give you another chance, Joey.'

Tina goes and kisses JFK again. 'Well?' Ruby says.

'It was you, Ruby, right?' JFK says. Everyone laughs.

'Wrong,' Ruby says. 'It was Tina.'

Out on the main floor, Miss Happyfeet is shouting, 'Texas two-step, everyone!'

Ruby says, 'Now we need a boy Ruler.'

'I'll go,' says Jessie. 'It's your party, Willa. You be the Mole.'

Oh no. I sit down in the centre. I pass on the goggles. Jessie ties the blindfold. This is embarrassing. I probably look stupid. Who is Jessie pointing to? What if Stella dances by? What if . . . and then there are lips on my cheek. I smell peppermint.

'Well?' Ruler Jessie asks. 'Who was it?'

The music is blasting and happy heels are pounding across the old barn floor, but nothing's beating louder than my heart. 'JFK,' I whisper.

'What?' Ruler Jessie shouts. 'We can't hear you.'

'It's Joseph. Final answer.'

'Right,' Jessie says. Someone takes off the blindfold.

I hear Stella. 'Willa? *Willa?*' Everybody stands up and shuffles around.

'There you are,' Stella says. Thankfully it's too

dark to see my face. 'Please come dance, Willa.
The party's almost over and you're going to insult
the Blazers if—'

'Sure, Mrs Gracemore,' Ruby says. 'We'll dance.
I love to dance. Come on, everybody. We're being
rude.'

We follow Ruler Ruby. My heart is still
pounding. I can still smell peppermint.

'There you are!' Miss Happyfeet says. 'Time for
a swing!'

JFK comes up beside me. 'Hey, Willa. I was
wondering if you want to go see a movie this
weekend. Jessie's asking Tina. And I thought
maybe we could . . .'

Yes. Finally. 'Sure, I'd like—'

And just then, Miss Happyfeet sweeps towards
us and pulls JFK on to the dance floor. She pulls
Ruby in to be his partner. JFK looks flustered.
Ruby looks thrilled.

'Don't worry, Joey,' I hear Ruby say. 'I learned
this at the club years ago.'

And then they are dancing. Ruby and JFK. And
they look great together. Why does JFK always
have to be such a good sport? Why can't he be

a jerk like some of the other . . . *Whoosh* . . . the barn door swings open.

In struts a girl tall as the Statue of Liberty. Gorgeous face, emerald green eyes, white curls cascading like waterfalls. She stands there as bright as the harvest moon in her white leather jacket and cowboy hat.

Feet stop. Eyes pop. Jaws drop. Someone says, 'Is she a ghost or for real?'

'Well, Hell-O, Bramble!' The apparition smiles, showing off dazzling white teeth. 'Am I too late for the party?'

'*Suzy-Jube!*' Mama B shrieks.

'*Suzy-Jube!*' Papa B echoes.

They race to hug her.

We stare speechless as the Blazers do their Pilgrim-Pochahontas-Moon dance. I couldn't even begin to paint you a picture.

'Am I too late?' Suzanna Jubilee says all excited and out of breath.

'Oh no,' Jessie shouts. He walks towards her like he's possessed.

'You're right on time,' Luke says, rushing forward. 'What a *fox* . . .'

Sam's eyes are dinner plates. Stella elbows him. 'We've got a holiday dinner to put on tomorrow,' she says. 'Let's start wrapping this up.'

'Hey, guys, wait,' Ruby says in a desperate voice. 'It's getting late and I almost forgot. We have to do the drawing for the Pats box seats.'

The boys aren't sure which way to turn. Fox? Football? Fox? Football?

'All right, NOW,' Ruby demands their attention. 'Super Bowl! Box seats!' She holds the basket with the names inside over her head. 'Pick one, Willa.'

I draw out a slip of paper, but before I can unfold it, Ruby pulls it from my hand.

'OK,' she says, 'the winner of the two box seats, compliments of the Sivler Family, to the Patriots Super Bowl game is . . .'

The boys crowd in.

'. . . Joey Kennelly.'

Ruby sticks the paper in the pocket of her jeans.

19

Grabbing the Glad

What is love? 'tis not hereafter;
Present mirth hath present laughter;
What's to come is still unsure:
In delay there lies no plenty;
Then come kiss me, sweet and twenty,
Youth's a stuff will not endure.

— **Shakespeare**, *Twelfth Night*

We made $1,300 at the Turkey Tango. The twenty-nine Blazers came in handy. There were even two unexplained Bens in the jar. Mama and Papa B, I bet. I knew we could do this! Just a few more successful events and we'll save the Bramble Library.

The good smells of Thanksgiving are wafting through the Inn. We're all just waiting for the turkey. Mama and Papa B invite me to play Monopoly. Suzy-Jube is 'catching up on her beauty sleep', Mama B explains. Papa B picks the top hat. Mama B picks the car. I pick the little dog that looks like Scamp.

The Blazers have a variation on the traditional Monopoly rules. Every time you pass go and collect $200, you have to put twenty bucks 'income tax' in the centre. If you land on 'Free Parking' you win it. 'Makes a nice year-end bonus,' Papa says.

When I land on Community Chest, I tell the Blazers about Sam's definition of Community Rent. The Blazers look at each other and smile.

'Reminds me of that quote you had up on your Bramble Board last month,' Mama B says. 'The one about spending yourself to get rich.' She winks at Papa B.

Gramp Tweed sits next to me at dinner. 'I'm going to try to see an old Doane Stuart chum of mine when Nana and I are in the City in a couple of weeks' time. Chas Butler is an old-school philanthropist. He's frugal unless he believes; but if he believes, he's Santa Claus. I think maybe he'll help the library campaign.'

'Is he from Bramble?' I figure only someone from Bramble would care.

'No,' Gramp says. 'But Chas loves books the way we love books.'

'Thanks so much, Gramp.' I hug him. 'Good luck making Santa believe.'

'Save some of that love for me,' Nana says to Gramp.

Gramp laughs and kisses Nana. 'Come on, Mrs Tweed. Time to go. We've got a big day tomorrow.'

Black Friday, the day after Thanksgiving, is the busiest day of the year for most retail stores. Everybody starts shopping for the holidays. Books and candy are popular presents. Nana and Gramp let me work in the store.

It's Friday so I check to see what Muffles is keeping warm. *A Christmas Memory*, by Truman Capote, and a book about writing, *Bird by Bird*.

'Capote's one of my favourites,' Gramp says. 'A *Christmas Memory* is a gem. And *Bird*, well, it's food for the writer's soul. I think you'll like it, Willa.'

'You haven't steered me wrong yet, Gramp. Thanks.'

It amazes me how Gramp knows just about every book in the store. And he knows his customers too. He asks Mrs Pasternack how her book club liked last month's selection. He hands a new mystery set at an opera house to Mrs DeBatista. She's a mystery buff and an opera lover. Gramp asks Mr Cohen if his grandson liked the book he suggested for his birthday. He shows Mr Tompkins a new fly-fishing title.

I don't know how Gramp keeps all those books and all those people in his head like that, but he does. And his customers trust him, just like people trust Mrs Saperstone. If they say a book is good, the book is good.

I'm helping a customer when I happen to look out and see JFK walk by across the street. A minute later I see Ruby. She crosses over and comes in.

'Oh, hi, Willa.' Ruby has a strange look on her face.

'Can I help you find something,' I ask.

'I'm good,' Ruby says. 'Hey, did you see the heart lockets at Wickstrom's?'

'No.' I turn a stack of new books by a favourite author face out on the shelf.

'You can open the heart,' Ruby says, 'and there's room inside for two tiny pictures, one on each side, you know . . . like for a girl and her boyfriend.'

'Willa,' Gramp calls, 'would you please wrap Mrs Miller's order?'

'Sure, Gramp.' When I finish, Ruby is gone.

Extra workers come in at four. Nana finishes refilling the Swedish fish bin and says, 'Come upstairs with me, Willa. I want to show you my new dress.'

It's black velvet with shiny silver beads around the neckline.

'After the show, Alexander's taking me to dinner and then dancing at the Rainbow Room.' Nana is so excited. 'Do you think it's fancy enough?'

'Oh, it's fancy, Nana. You look beautiful. Gramp's a lucky guy. And I'm proud of you for walking every day.'

'I've lost nine pounds,' Nana says, 'and I feel ten years younger.' Her happy face saddens a bit. 'I know Stella thinks we're foolish driving off-Cape in the winter at our age, during our busiest season, no less. You know how Stella feels about business. But you only live once, right? You've got to grab the glad while you can.'

Suzanna Jubilee's Advice

For such as I am all true lovers are:
Unstaid and skittish in all motions else
Save in the constant image of the creature
*   that is belov'd.*

— **The Poet of Love,** *Twelfth Night*

I wake up Saturday to the sun streaming through my window. It's going to be a beautiful day. After brunch I finish my homework and then head downstairs to talk to Suzanna. There are Blazers everywhere, grabbing the glad where they can. Charades in the living room. Poker in the den. Mama and Papa B are dozing by the fireplace. As I pass by, Papa snorts and they wake up.

'Suzy's tummy's a bit crummy,' Papa B says, patting his paunch in solidarity.

'No reflection on the food, of course,' Mama B says. 'Everything here is just delicious, honey. Your daddy's an excellent cook. It's just that Suzy-Jube's been eating like a bird for the pageants, but here, the temptations were just too great.'

I did see Suzanna tackling the bacon station three times this morning.

Mama B smooths the spot next to her. 'Sit a bit.' I do. Papa B sits on my other side. I'm trapped between friendly bears. Mama B lifts a thick album off the table. 'This gives us a chance to brag a bit anyhoo. Let's look-see Suzy-Jube's modelling album. Your mama saw it earlier and she said to be sure to show you too.'

'Oh, great,' I say. Thanks a lot, Stella.

Chickles opens to a bald-headed baby who looks like every other bald-headed baby. She turns a few pages. Now Suzanna has a huge wisp of white hair sticking up straight on her head like a duck. I dig my fingernails in.

'And here's Suzy-Jube when she was three,' Chickles says.

I keep checking the clock as we travel on. On and on and on.

Suzanna in a pink tutu, blue tutu, new braces, sparkly cape, purple gown, yellow gown . . . I smile and nod while inside I'm thinking about JFK. The peppermint kiss and the almost invitation to the movies and was that really his name Ruby picked for the Pat box seats and why hasn't Ruby mentioned her date with Chris Ruggiero and what if she likes JFK again and what's with the whole heart-locket thing? I need to call Tina.

'And here she is today,' Papa B says.

Suzanna Jubilee is wearing a red bathing suit with a 'Miss Brewer County' sash and tiara. She looks like Marilyn Monroe, shapely and gorgeous, with those white waterfall curls. I bet Suzanna has no trouble getting any boy she likes.

'Isn't she a beauty?' Papa B says in a quivering voice. 'And she's the sweetest, nicest girl you'd ever meet.'

'Beautiful inside and out,' Mama B says. 'And our baby girl's gonna be the next Miss Daisydew USA. If she can just work on her talent.'

Yes, finally I'll find out. 'What exactly is Suzanna's tal—'

'Now, Mama, stop.' Suzanna walks in. 'I don't

want to hear another word about the talent portion of the competition. It's just one eensy-weensy little part of the scoring and I've been practising, hard. You'll jinx me if you keep on—'

'Won't mention it again, sugar plum,' Mama B says.

'Not a word,' Papa B promises.

Oh, please, I'm dying to know.

'Hello, Willa,' Suzanna says, looking at me. 'Such a pretty little thing.'

I pull my shoulders back and stick out my chest.

'I'd love to see the ocean up here,' Suzanna says.

'Oh, sure,' I say, 'let's go.' I've been hoping for a chance to talk to her.

It's warm so we grab two bikes from the shed. 'The beach is close,' I say.

People stop and stare as we go by. A boy rides his bike smack into a tree. A man in a jeep swerves up on the kerb, just missing a telephone pole.

Suzanna laughs. 'Don't worry, Willa. Happens everywhere I go.'

Nature's not immune to Suzy-Jube's charms

either. At Sandy Beach, the wind whistles loudly and gulls collide in the air. Fish leap up on the sand to see her. The tide rushes in . . . and stops.

I wonder what JFK thought of her?

'Who's that handsome curly-haired boy you were with at the turkey dance?' Suzanna says.

'I wasn't with him. We were all just hanging out as friends.'

Suzanna laughs. 'Honey, I can spot lovin' eyes a hundred miles away. You couldn't take your baby blues off that boy and he couldn't keep his off you either.'

'I don't know, Suzanna. I'm so confused.'

'Good,' she says. 'If it ain't confusing, it ain't much fun.'

'But you see, there's this other girl—'

'The redhead with the big moo-mas?'

'Ruby,' I say, and laugh. Suzanna laughs too.

'I saw her,' she says. 'But she can't hold a candle to you, honey.'

'Well, it's just that I think Ruby likes JFK too.'

'His name is J-F-K?' Suzanna gushes. 'I just love a man with initials.'

'And I think Ruby finagled it so that JFK won

a trip to the Super Bowl with her in her family's private jet—'

'Whoa there,' Suzanna says. 'Money can't buy love, suga'. Not true love. If you want that boy, you've got to learn his heart.'

'What?'

'You've got to find out what he loves. Maybe it's a sport, or he's got some big dream . . . Find out what he loves and then show him you think it's the most fascinating thing since the invention of cotton candy.'

'But what if I don't like the things he likes most?'

'Don't worry, Willa girl. You don't look at someone the way you two were looking at each other if you don't already know your hearts match.'

The stretch-limos with 'Blazin', Blazin', it's amazin'' slogans painted on the sides pull up after dinner on Sunday. After Suzanna Jubilee's Daisydew USA pageant next weekend, they're off to Paris for Christmas and then to their California house for the Miss American Role Model preliminaries.

There's a whole lot of hugging and promises to be back in the spring.

What does JFK love? I wonder as I write in my diary. I know he likes football. I know he likes rap music. But those are just things. I wonder what he really *cares about* inside. I wonder what he wants to be. I wonder if he has a dream . . .

21

Winter Vacation Plans

Did my heart love till now? forswear it, sight!
For I ne'er saw true beauty till this night.

– Shakespeare, *Romeo and Juliet*

Community Service meets after school. Plans
for the 'Summer in the Snow Beach Party' are
swimming along nicely.

'Sam is renting extra space heaters and getting
sand for the floor,' I say.

'Daddy knows the owner of the new Roche
Brothers market,' Tina says. 'I'll see if they'll donate
the hotdogs and hamburgers.'

JFK, Jessie and Luke come in. 'Where's your
new friend, Willa?' Luke asks.

He means Suzanna Jubilee.

'Her family left,' I say. 'They were just visiting.'

Jessie and Luke look distraught.

'But it's good you're here,' I say. 'We're making plans for the next fundraising event. A Summer in the Snow Beach Party in the barn.'

'My uncle's best friend is a DJ,' JFK says. 'He might do the gig for free. I'll call him tonight.' JFK hasn't said another word about the movies.

'And Luke and I'll play free too,' Jessie volunteers.

What's a beach party without buoys? Tina and I look at each other and smile.

'And how about a snowman contest?' I say. 'If we have enough snow.'

'We'll be in our bathing suits, Willa,' Tina reminds me.

'Oooh, nice,' Jessie says. Tina punches his arm and giggles.

Oh no, bathing suits. How could I forget? I'd much rather be in a ski jacket, outside making snowmen, than dancing in a bathing suit next to Tina and Ruby.

We move on to the Midwinter Night's Dream. The boys groan. 'Just give me a job later,' JFK says to me as they leave.

'The gym is reserved and I'm working on a band,' Ruby says. 'Committee members, why don't you give your reports?'

Trish and Emily got all the paper goods donated. Lauren says decorations are under control. Caroline found a florist. Alexa says Mama Java's is supplying coffee and Kelsey's sending home a flyer asking parents to make fancy desserts.

'OK, girls, listen to this!' Tina is dying to share her matchmaking questionnaire. She's been working on it night and day.

'One. What's your favourite food?
    Two. What's your favourite pizza topping?
    Three. What's your favourite dessert?'

'Are all the questions about food?' I ask.
    'Food's important, Willa. Especially to boys.

'Four. What's your favourite candy?
    Five. What's your favourite ice cream? I mean the actual cold stuff—'

'Oh, come on, Tina—' I say.

'Six. What's your favourite TV show?

Seven. What's your all-time favourite movie?

Eight. What's your favourite team?

Nine. What's your favourite Cape beach?

Ten. What's your favourite gum?

And I'm still working on a tie-breaker . . .'

'I've got an idea,' I say, but Tina and Ruby are late for nail appointments. 'Same time next week,' I say. I check with Mr Kay about an Algebra question then head to the lab to finish a science report. It's getting dark by the time I leave school.

Outside I look up. The first star tonight. *I wish I may, I wish I might* . . . I turn the corner towards the bike racks and there is JFK. Sitting on the bench by the willow tree. He's writing fast and furiously, like he's got an idea that he doesn't want to lose.

I know that feeling. I wait until he's finished. 'Hi, Joseph.'

'Willa, hi.' He closes the notebook.

'Homework?' I ask.

'Yeah, no . . . lyrics.'

'Can I hear them?' I say. I sit down next to him on the bench.

He looks at me. 'I guess so.' He opens the notebook. 'Here, you can read it.'

Winter Vacation Plans

'*rich burb mommas strategizing, private bay or ocean side?*
poor kerb mommas agonizing, medicine or heat or fries?
winter vacation plans

'Wow, Joseph. This is rap? This is good. Really good.'

'You like it?' He smiles.

'I love it. "Winter Vacation Plans." Great title. What got you writing this?'

'I don't know,' JFK says. 'It just bothers me that some people are mega rich and other people can't even buy their kids decent food or medicine when they're sick. It's not right. My mom volunteers at this homeless shelter in Hyannis and I help her sometimes. I thought it would just be old drunks. But no, lots of times it's mothers with little kids who got evicted from their apartments or their husbands beat them up and they're scared . . .'

Wow, I had no idea he cared about these things. Important things. Not only is JFK beautiful on the outside, he's beautiful on the inside too. If I ever had one smidgen of doubt, I don't any more. I am totally in love with this boy.

'And it's funny,' JFK says, 'but reading Shakespeare's been good for my lyrics. I know everybody in class thinks his stories are lame, but that guy could groove. He had a mean rhythm. He'd have made a great rapper.'

'Well maybe you could help Shakespeare get his groove back.'

'Yeah, maybe,' JFK says. He laughs. 'Right after I end world hunger.'

I write in my journal and then open Shakespeare to *The Winter's Tale*:

'When you do dance, I wish you a wave o' the sea,
that you might ever do nothing but that.'

I imagine Shakespeare standing on a beach. He lived on an island, England, of course. I look out at the same ocean he did. And I can tell he loved nature.

'Here's flowers for you . . . lavender . . . marigold . . .;
daffodils, that come before the swallow dares, and take
the winds of March with beauty.'

He talks so much about the wind, I'm certain Shakespeare knew that feeling of the sea wind whistling through your ears, walking until your worries wash away and your heart is light and happy.

'Jog on, jog on, the footpath way, and merrily hent the
stile-a;
Your merry heart goes all the day, Your sad tires in a
mile-a.'

That passage always makes me smile-a. Some day I'll see the Globe Theatre and visit the places that inspired old Will. Maybe JFK will come with me.

Shakespeare talks so much about love. It seems that word is in everything he wrote. *'I love a ballad* in print . . .' he said. Me too, Will, me too. Some day, I want to be a writer. But like you say in *The Winter's Tale* . . . *'there's time enough for that.'*

22

Sing It, Sister!

Some say that ever 'gainst that season comes
Wherein our Saviour's birth is celebrated,
The bird of dawning singeth all night long:
And then, they say, no spirit can walk abroad;
The nights are wholesome; then no planets strike,
No fairy takes, nor witch hath power to charm,
So hallow'd and so gracious is the time.

                                           – Shakespeare, *Hamlet*

We do a lot of celebrating at BUC in December. Hanukkah, Christmas, Diwali, Kwanzaa . . . Mum starts the month off with a candlelight service. The room is packed.

'Nearly all the world's great religions speak of light this season,' Mum says. 'The oil lamps of Hanukkah, the star over Bethlehem . . .'

As Mum talks, she lights a candle. She walks slowly down the aisle, stopping to light the candle of each person on the end of a row. Those people then turn and light the candles of the people next to them, and on and on and on. I wave to Mrs Saperstone across the aisle. Dr Swammy is sitting next to her. Too bad Nana and Gramp are missing this, but I'm sure they're having a great time in New York.

Mum lights my candle. It flickers and sputters. I light Sam's candle. Sam turns towards Stella. Soon, everyone's face is aglow. I see JFK with his family a few rows back. He raises his candle. I raise mine back.

Mum starts singing. It's Gramp's favourite song and mine. We all join in:

'*This little light of mine, I'm gonna let it shine,*
Oh, this little light of mine, I'm gonna let it shine.'

'Sing it, sister!' a man's voice bellows, and we all turn back to look.

A tall black man in a grey suit and fancy hat is walking up the aisle. He manoeuvres a cane in one hand. There's a bouquet of flowers in the other.

The man is smiling like he just saw Jesus. He's heading straight towards Mum.

'This little light of mine . . .'

Even in the dark, I can see that the stranger is handsome, very handsome. He walks with a confident swagger, like he's walked up this aisle a hundred times before, although clearly, he's not from Bramble.

I look at Mum. She's stopped singing. Her hands are clasped over her mouth. Tears are streaming down her face. Her whole body is shaking.

We keep singing for her. *'I'm gonna let it shine . . .'*

When the stranger reaches Mum, he stops. He holds out the bouquet. 'Sully?'

'*Riley!*' Mum screams and falls into his arms.

'Let it shine, let it shine, let it shine.'

After the service JFK asks me, 'Want to see a movie Friday?'

'Sure,' I say, still sort of weepy over watching Mum and her long-lost love. Cupid came through after all. 'Are Jessie and Tina coming too?'

'No,' JFK says. 'Not unless you want them too.'

Out of the corner of my eye I spot Ruby staring at us.

'I thought maybe just the two of us could go,' JFK says a bit awkwardly.

'I'd love to,' is all I have the chance to say before Stella calls me to go.

I can't write in my diary fast enough:

A date Friday . . . then the Beach Party Saturday . . . two nights in a row. Thank you!

23

So Quick Bright Things . . .

So quick bright things come to confusion . . .

– Shakespeare, *A Midsummer Night's Dream*

I run to my locker in the morning. I can't wait to tell Tina. She'll know exactly what I should wear on my first 'just-the-two-of-us' date with JFK. I still haven't asked Stella if I can go yet, but everything feels so perfect, somehow I'm not worried.

The Burners are huddled around Ruby. I can tell Ruby sees me coming.

'Oh, it's beautiful,' one of the Burners squeals.

'What did he say when he gave it to you?' another Burner shrieks.

Ruby whispers something and they all giggle.

'Oh, hi, Willa,' Ruby says loudly, like she

just noticed me. She is twisting something shiny around her neck.

'Show her,' one of the Burners says. She's talking about me.

'No,' Ruby says, but I can tell she really wants to.

'What is it?' I ask, taking the bait.

'A locket,' Ruby says, showing me the silver chain with a heart in the middle.

'Open it,' one of the Burners says.

'Yes, show her,' another Burner says.

Ruby opens the heart and I bend in closer to see.

Ruby's picture is on one side. JFK's on the other.

'He picked it out for her,' one of the Burners says.

The room is swirling. I can't breathe. *It can't possibly be.*

Then with an icy shiver I remember seeing JFK in town on Black Friday. And then Ruby came in the store talking about the new necklaces at Wickstrom's . . .

'Got to go,' I manage to say. 'I'm late.'

I run outside. I can't go to class. There's the bench by the willow where he showed me his lyrics. The tears start. 'Miss Havisham, you'll be late,' Mademoiselle Ferret snaps, rushing past. The bell rings and I turn to follow, but my whole body's shaking, *no*.

I run down to the basement, to the bathroom by the old art studio. *How could you do this to me, JFK?* You just asked me out on a date! And Ruby said she liked Chris Ruggerio. I hate you Ruby. It smells like urine and turpentine in here. I'm going to puke. I'm not going back upstairs ever. I slide down on the floor and cry.

I cry through first bell and the second and then I turn from sad to mad. *Get up Willa, grow up.* He had no right to treat you like that. Track him down. You deserve an explanation. You told Mum to be a leaper. Be a leaper yourself, Willa. Come on.

I wash my face, fix my hair and charge upstairs like a nor'easter. At the landing I turn, huffing, and that's when I see Stella and Sam. They are standing in front of Headmaster Chillmark's office. What's up? My grades are great. Dr Chillmark pats Stella's back awkwardly, as if he's trying to comfort her. He shakes Sam's hand.

'Mother? Sam?' I walk towards them. I have a sick feeling inside. When they turn, I can tell by their faces, my life is about to change. I freeze like a statue.

Stella bursts into tears. Sam grips her arm. They walk slowly towards me.

Nana.

Oh no, please God, not Nana.

'No,' I say loudly, shaking my head.

Stella and Sam move faster.

'No!' I shout. Nana was walking every day. She . . .

Kids stop in the hall to watch. Sam and Stella are nearly to me.

'It's OK, Willa,' Sam says. 'We just need to talk to you . . .'

'No, no, no,' I start crying. *Not Nana, not Nana, please.*

Stella reaches me first and wraps me in a hug. She whispers gently in my ear. 'No, sweetheart. Nana's fine.'

24

Goodnight, Sweet Prince

Now cracks a noble heart.
Good night, sweet prince,
And flights of angels sing thee to thy rest . . .
— **Shakespeare**, *Hamlet*

On the morning of Gramp's wake, it started to snow. Thick and heavy, like sheets of fog, sweeping in off the ocean. It snowed all day and by 4 p.m., when calling hours at McNulty Funeral Home officially started, there was more than a foot and a half. It seemed it would never stop.

But the snow didn't stop Alexander Tweed's many friends from coming.

The line of mourners started at the steps of McNulty's and curved around to High Street, up and over the snow banks to Foster, around Tudor and Guilder and Starboard, and all the way to Main Street, where candles and bears and bouquets of flowers graced the steps of Sweet Bramble Books.

Gramp Tweed died of a heart attack in New York City. It happened quickly. He didn't suffer much. There wasn't time for us to get to the hospital.

And here all this time I was worried about Nana. I am frozen. I cannot cry.

It hit me like a glacier when I first saw Nana after Gramp's death, that in all the years I have seen Nana laugh, I have never seen her cry.

Now she cannot stop.

At first Nana wouldn't answer the door. 'Please, Mother,' Stella begged in the gentlest voice I've ever heard her use. Scamp was barking and scratching against the door, Muffles purring strangely. 'Please, Mother, let me in.' Stella pressed her ear to the door for an answer. 'It's OK, Mother, I know. We just want to help.'

When Nana screamed, '*Get away from me,*' Stella told Sam to take me home.

Sam nodded. I didn't argue.

The next morning I overheard Stella telling

Sam how she found a spare key in the store. Upstairs, Nana was curled up on the kitchen floor, shivering, Scamp and Muffles worried sick by her side.

I wasn't there but I can imagine how it went. 'It was my fault, my fault,' Nana had sobbed. 'We never should have gone to New—'

'No, Mother,' Stella said, holding Nana in her arms like a baby, kissing her soft wrinkled cheek. 'It's OK, Mother, it's OK . . .' Nana cried and cried and Stella didn't rush her. Later, Stella helped Nana take a bath. She warmed up some soup and fed it to her slowly. She covered Nana with quilts on the couch and stayed up all night in the chair beside her, in case her mother needed anything.

Many people want to 'say a few words' about Gramp. Mum welcomes each one to the microphone. Stella never leaves Nana's side. She hands her tissues and holds her arm firmly, so strong and kind and gentle.

'He was our town psychologist,' Gramp's friend Bill Carroll says. 'When my Mary died after thirty-two years of marriage and nobody knew what to do, Alexander brought me a bag of books that got me through that winter.'

'He never judged anybody,' Mrs Bellimo said with a hiccup.

Mr Cohen goes next. 'When my grandson announced he hated reading, Alexander said, 'Here David, give him this one. "Maniac something" I think it was called. Now Sammy can't read a book fast enough.'

One after the other, my Gramp's customers, my Gramp's friends, stood up and talked about him. And nearly every one of them mentioned a book.

Mrs Saperstone hugs me. 'See how personal books are, Willa? Your Gramp gave these people books that gave them hope and they will never forget him.'

Dr Swaminathan shares something from Shakespeare about a sweet prince with a noble heart. Yes, that was my Gramp.

Sam reads from the poet Emily Dickinson:

We never know how high we are till we are called to rise;
And then, if we are true to plan, our statures touch the
*   skies.*

'Alexander,' Sam's voice breaks, 'Alexander Tweed was a tall, tall man.'

Mum reads the 'love is patient, love is kind' passage from the Bible, then leads us in Gramp's favourite song, 'This little light of mine, I'm gonna let it shine . . .'

Stella, I am certain, wanted to say something, but Nana needed her daughter by her side and Stella stayed rock-sturdy by her, never faltering for a second.

I went last.

'My Gramp and I loved to talk about books. Every Friday he'd have a new one picked out specially, just for me. We'd drink lemon tea and talk about the stories, what made us laugh and cry. I realize now we weren't just talking about books on those Friday afternoons. We were talking about life.

'William Shakespeare once said, "*We know what we are, but know not what we may be.*" I know this for sure. I am my grandfather's granddaughter, and whatever I will be, whatever I will do in my life, his spirit will shine on in me.'

*

It's a long evening as people come through the receiving line, saying kind words to Nana and Stella and Sam and me. Tina is the first of my friends in line, her face wet with tears. She hugs me tight. 'If there's anything I can do for you, sweetie. *Anything*. You just call me.'

'I'm sorry, Tina, but we're going to have to cancel the Beach Party.'

'Of course, Willa, we know. Don't worry. I'll take care of everything.'

The workers from Sweet Bramble Books come through and all the staff from the Inn. My teachers, our neighbours. *Where is JFK?*

Emily, Trish, Lauren and Kelsey. *Where is he?* Jessie and Luke and Lexy and Caroline, even Ruby Sivler and her parents, *where is . . .*

And then, I see him. JFK. At the end of the line, covered with snow.

'It was a very long line out there,' Stella whispers in my ear.

He came. I'm so confused. Thoughts from my head and thoughts from my heart converge like the currents at the tip of the Spit. Does he like me or does he like Ruby? He's here, but why did he give Ruby the locket?

By the time he reaches me, the snow has melted and JFK is dripping wet. He looks like a golden-haired shaggy dog with very, very blue eyes. He's wearing his Bramble uniform. JFK got dressed up for my Gramp.

There will be time for explanations later. What matters now is that he is here.

'I'm sorry, Willa.' His lip trembles. 'Come here,' he says. He hugs me.

And thankfully, at last, I cry.

25

The Sign

If ever thou shalt love,
In the sweet pangs of it remember me . . .

– Shakespeare, *Twelfth Night*

On Friday, after the funeral, everyone comes back to the Inn for lunch. I try to be cheerful for Nana and helpful for Stella. I try to listen to the kind things people say, not remembering a word of it. I am in a dream, a horrible dream.

It's always sad when someone dies, but, until you lose someone you love, really love, you don't know how much it hurts.

The next morning I'm in the kitchen making tea, when Stella comes in.

'Want to go for a run with me,' she asks. 'I think the roads are clear now.'

Stella never asks me to run with her. She likes
to go alone.

'Sure,' I say. 'Just let me get dressed.'

We jog towards town. We don't say a word as
we pass Sweet Bramble Books. There's a stunning
red cardinal on the tree out front. It looks at me as
we go by.

'To the beach?' Stella shouts.

'Sure,' I say. And then we don't talk any
more.

It's so cold, we make ghosts in the air as we
breathe. I push myself to keep up with Stella. I'm
a pretty strong runner from soccer, but Stella's
much faster than me.

After a bit, Stella slows down and adjusts her
pace to mine. We are nearly to Sandy Beach. I
turn towards Stella to say something, but then
I see her face. My mother looks calm, peaceful.
The way Sam looks on his bench in the labyrinth.
The way Mum looks at BUC. I smile and zip my
lips. It's enough just to be with her.

Later, after lunch, I get on my boots. Sam cleared
the labyrinth path yesterday. I brush snow from the

statue of the girl reading a book. Stella and Sam brought it back for me from their honeymoon on Nantucket. The weekend after Nana and Gramp got married. Everything was perfect then. My four favourite people were in love.

Sam is sitting on the old stone bench in the middle of the labyrinth. His eyes are closed. I walk quietly so I won't disturb him.

The holly-berry bushes are in bloom. The ground is frozen but clear of brush. Sam takes good care of this circle. I bend down for a sprig of lavender, rub the green needles between my fingers and sniff. *Hmmm*. Nana's favourite flower. Gramp wore a boutonnière of lavender from this garden on their Valentine's wedding day. 'Good thing about lavender,' Sam said then, 'it blooms again and again.'

I throw the sprig down. I kick a stump. *How could you do this? Why Gramp?*

A cardinal lands on a branch before me. It looks like the one I saw earlier. The red is bright against the grey. The bird looks at me, *hurrgh, hurrgh*, then flies off.

I take a deep breath and let it out. I take another

and another. The labyrinth path loops me inwards and then away as I circle towards the centre.

After a while, as I walk, I am more peaceful inside. The red bird comes back. *Hello.* I keep on breathing and walk, feeling better as I go.

When I reach the bench, Sam sees me and smiles. I sit and lean my head on his arm. His wool sweater is scratchy. Neither of us wants to talk.

The red cardinal comes again. It looks at me, *hurrgh, hurrgh,* and it's off.

That night as I write in my journal, I think about my day. The run with Stella. The labyrinth with Sam. The stunning red cardinal. And as I write it strikes me. I start laughing through my tears. *Thank you,* Gramp. Thanks for the sign. Hearts heal and love lives on. *Bird by bird, buddy. Bird by bird.*

26

Making Santa Believe

Thy sweet love remember'd such wealth brings . . .

— Shakespeare, *Sonnet 29*

When Nana sent Gramp's obituary notice to the *Cape Cod Times*, she wrote, 'In lieu of flowers, and in honour of Alexander's great love of books, the family invites friends to send memorial contributions to the 'Save the Bramble Library' fund c/o First United Bank of Bramble, Cape Cod, Massachusetts.

Alexander Tweed had a lot of friends. Cheques poured in over Christmas like tourists across the Bourne Bridge on the fourth of July. Fifty dollars. One hundred dollars. Five hundred dollars. Six dollars and twenty-five cents from Mr Cohen's grandson.

And then early in January, by special delivery, a letter came addressed to me from Charles Noble Butler III, New York, New York. Gramp's old school buddy, 'Chas.'

$10,000.

I run in to the kitchen, smack into Stella. 'Mother, we've got it. Ten thousand dollars. That's more than we need now!'

'Hoorah!' Stella says. She lifts me up and swirls me around.

'What's all the commotion,' Sam says, rushing in.

'We did it!' I'm dancing my nose in the air Snoopy dance. 'Gramp made Santa believe. Just wait until Mrs Saperstone hears!'

Sam and Stella are laughing, they're so happy for me.

But then I think of something. I stop dancing. 'It's sort of cheating how we got the money, though. We were supposed to earn it.'

'You did, Willa', Stella says, clenching my arm. 'You absolutely did. I learned this in my MBA course on development at NYU. There are two major kinds of philanthropy. There's *fund*-raising and then there's *friend*-raising. The first is good, but the second is more powerful. Your Gramp believed in you so much that he convinced his friend Chas to believe. And who knows who Chas will influence? When you friend-raise the goodwill just keeps on spreading.'

I smile at my mother. I hug her. 'Thanks, Mom.'

On the way to the library, I see Ruby. We walk along Main Street. I tell her the good news. Ruby stares at me funny. I think she's going to cry or something.

'You're so lucky, Willa,' she says. 'You're smart and pretty and people really like you. There's something different about you too. Like caring so much about saving the library . . .' She shakes her head. 'I wish I . . .' Ruby stops in front of the new Sea Spa. She looks at her watch. 'Well, anyway. I'm late for my seaweed wrap.'

Ruby thinks I'm lucky? She actually sounded jealous of me. What a surprise. But it's Mrs Saperstone who is in for the really big surprise.

*

The closed sign is up but the door is open. I burst in shouting the news.

Mrs Saperstone is standing by the window, wearing her coat. There are boxes everywhere. Outside, the whale fountain is covered with snow.

'We raised all the money. Even more than we needed! I don't know how much total, but it's way more than the ten thousand dollars the council said we—'

'Willa.' Mrs Saperstone puts a book in a box. She shakes her head. She sits down. 'I don't know how to tell you this . . .' Her lips tighten as she hands me a letter.

It's from Mr Sivler, on behalf of the town council. 'It seems we have miscalculated the extent of the library's financial dilemma. The situation is significantly more dire than originally projected . . .'

Now they need $25,000 by the fifteenth of February.

'No,' I say, my heart pounding. 'They can't do this. That's not fair!'

*

I'm late for our Community Service meeting. I bound into the room with the news about the increase. Only a few of the girls are there and none of the boys. 'We can't let the council get away with this,' I say. 'We're going to have to double our goal for January and I think maybe we'll have to increase ticket prices for the February dance –' I stop when I realize that nobody is listening. And where are all the boys? 'Come on, everybody. Let's do the Bowling for Books idea for January.'

Tina and Ruby look at each other. They don't like bowling.

'You know, Willa,' Tina says, 'I think we should skip it. Let's focus on making the Dream a huge hit.'

'I've even got the Mashpee Common Great Room for free instead of the gym,' Ruby says. 'It can hold five hundred people. And Mommy's flying in her friend, Shirley Katz, from Manhattan, to consult on decorations and food. Shirley plans A-list events for the Trumps and . . .'

After school, I stop by Mum's. From the porch I hear music, a man's voice, Mum's chuckle.

'Willa, what a nice surprise,' Mum says. 'How are you holding up? And how's your Nana doing?'

'We're hanging in there,' I say.

'Come on in, honey. I want you to meet someone.'

The stranger from BUC is sitting in Mum's kitchen. Mum's favourite singer, Billie Holliday, is playing. '*It had to be you . . .*' Something smells delicious.

'Willa, this is Riley Truth. Riley, this is my good friend Willa Havisham.'

Riley stands and shakes my hand. 'Pleasure to meet you, Willa. Sully's told me all about you. I'm sorry to hear of your loss.'

The oven buzzes. 'Good,' Mum says, 'pie's ready. You're just in time Willa.'

'Let me get that, princess,' Mr Truth says, 'you visit with your pretty young friend.' He pulls out a chair for me.

Princess? He calls Mum princess? Mum laughs. 'Thank you kindly, Ry.'

There's a green album on the table. 'Our high-school yearbook,' Mum says. 'Lord, didn't that bring back memories, Ry?'

'Surely did, Sully. Surely did.'

I open the book and begin turning pages. Every face is black. So different from Bramble. I wonder how Mum feels looking out at all that white every weekend? I wonder if she misses . . .

'She was my best friend,' Mum says, pointing to a beautiful girl with braids swooped into a band on the side of her head. 'Remember Zenobia Portee, Buck?'

'*Hmmm, hmmm*,' Riley says, 'give me a second . . . no . . . don't believe I even need a second, *hmmm, hmmm, hmmm*, ain't no man in the great state of South Carolina ever gonna forget Zenobia Portee. *Hmmm, hmmm,* was that girl a sight—'

'That's enough, old man,' Mum says, with a laugh.

'Show me your picture, Mum,' I say.

Mum flips back the pages. She points to a skinny girl with a mad look on her face. 'Why didn't you smile?' I ask.

'Let's just say I didn't like the *attitude* of the photographer,' Mum says.

Riley gets a fit of laughing that ends in a fit of coughing. 'Oh, Sully, you slay me, you do.'

On the way home, I pass by Hairs to You, and our hairdresser, Jo, comes out. 'Willa, wait.' She puffs my curly side. 'Nice. I like it. Can I take a picture?'

'Why?' I say with a laugh.

'For the stylists' album. Another girl just came in asking for "the Willa".'

'You're kidding.' I laugh.

'No really,' Jo says, snapping a picture. 'Everybody's asking for it.'

There's a sale sign in the window of Wickstrom's jewellery store. My birthday's next week. The thirteenth of January. I've been hinting for a watch. I go in to take a look.

The next case over is necklaces. I spot the heart lockets. A silver one with a tiny gold bow on top catches my eye. *So pretty*. Then I see the one JFK bought for Ruby. I feel like a boxer punched my stomach. How could JFK do that to me?

Mr Wickstrom sees me looking. 'Would you like to try one on?'

'No . . . yes . . . thanks.' I point to the silver heart with the gold bow on top.

'Lovely choice,' Mr Wickstrom says, 'elegant and classic.'

I open the locket and stare at the two empty hearts. I picture me on one side, JFK on the other. I hear the store door open, Mr Wickstrom greeting customers.

'Hey, Willa.' It can't be. JFK is there with his father and little brother.

'Hi, Joseph.' I quickly hand the necklace back to Mr Wickstrom.

'We're picking up my mother's birthday present,' JFK says.

'That's nice. Hi, Mr Kennelly. Hi, Brendan.'

'Are you buying a heart necklace too?' Joseph asks.

'What? No. Why?' My face flushes.

'Those lockets,' JFK says, pointing. 'I was in here with Dad ordering my mom's birthday gift, and Ruby Sivler came in. She said she couldn't decide which locket she liked best and could I please help her choose. I pointed to one, I'm not even sure which, and she was all happy because I helped her decide.'

Oh thank you, thank you. So JFK didn't buy a

locket for Ruby after all!

'No,' I say. 'I'm not buying one.' I start to leave, then stop. Be a leaper, Willa, leap. I fluff up my curly side, turn around and smile. 'A girl doesn't buy a locket for herself, Joseph. She gets one from a boy.'

27

Happy Birthday

There was a star danced,
And under that was I born.

– Shakespeare, *Much Ado About Nothing*

On my fourteenth birthday I build two snow people next to the Bramble Board. One's a bit taller. They are facing each other. I give them crazy pine-bough hair and set the stick arms so it looks like they're dancing.

Mother and Sam have a fancy dinner for me in the private dining room. Tina is invited, of course, and Nana, Mum and Riley, Dr Swammy and Mrs Saperstone.

Sam serves my favourites. Shrimp cocktail, Caesar salad, filet mignon and garlic mashed potatoes. Nana proposes a toast, like Gramp would have, but when she starts crying, Sam finishes. 'To our wonderful Willa. May this year be your happiest yet.'

'Cheers!'

Tina says she has a 'surprise' for me. Some friends are getting together.

It's freezing outside and dark, but the sky is bright with stars. I'm wearing the new sweater Nana bought me, the new earrings from Mum and the watch from Stella and Sam. I can't wait to see JFK.

Everyone's waiting for us at the bowling alley. Tina arranged the whole thing. Trish, Kelsey and Caroline, Emily, Allison, and Lexy, even Luke and Jessie. Everyone except JFK. JFK and Ruby.

'I think Ruby probably came down with that flu that's going around,' Tina says.

There is no flu going around.

'Oh yeah, Willa,' Jessie says. 'Joe said to tell you he's sorry but he had to go somewhere with his family tonight.'

'No problem.' I feel like someone dropped a bowling ball on my stomach.

Tina, in perfect best-friend form, makes it seems like bowling is the best sport ever. She gives me a card that everyone signed. Everyone except Ruby and JFK. There's a cheque inside made out to the Save the Bramble Library Fund.

'Instead of getting you a bunch of stuff you don't want – you are the most unmaterialistic person we know, Willa – we decided to put our money together and make a donation in your name to the library.'

'Thanks, everybody,' I say. 'This is great.'

Tina brings out a cake with a mermaid wearing a yellow bikini and sunglasses. I count the fourteen candles in my head. All my friends sing 'Happy Birthday', but the person I want most to be singing isn't even here. *Where is he?*

Tina hands me a knife. 'Don't forget to make a wish.'

I didn't forget. I close my eyes. The wishing part is easy.

Later as we're walking home, I hear Jessie and Luke talking. '. . . box seats for the Super Bowl, right over the fifty-yard line. How awesome is that? And they're flying him to Florida in their private jet. Her father is loaded . . .'

I forgot all about the Pats.

28

'The Boy-cott'

Young Adam Cupid, he that shot so trim
When King Cophetua lov'd the beggar maid.

– Shakespeare, Romeo and Juliet

'We have a huge problem,' Tina says at the Community Service meeting.

Only the girls are here. The boys have all dropped out. 'We've sold a hundred and two tickets for Dream.'

'*A hundred and two tickets*,' I say. 'That's great!'

'But only two of them are *boys*,' Tina says. 'We've got a hundred girls out there shopping for gowns and only two *boys* renting tuxedos. We didn't want to upset you with this before now, Willa, with your grandfather and all, and then it was your birthday, but we've got to do something, quick. The boys are boycotting the Dream!'

'We need a big draw,' Emily says. 'Something like Ruby's Super Bowl tick—'

Tina elbows Emily and gives her an evil look. I sneak a peek at Ruby. She looks at me. We both look somewhere else.

Update . . . JFK went to the Super Bowl with the Sivlers. What Patriots-loving boy in his right mind would pass up a chance like that? What Ruby didn't plan on, however, was that JFK gave the second ticket to his father. And they didn't fly down in the Sivler's private jet. JFK's Florida grandparents had invited the Kennellys for a January vacation and so JFK and his father were already going to be there. They just met up with the Sivlers at the stadium. Love those Florida grandparents.

'Kiss and Guess was a big hit at the turkey thing,' Tina says.

'Well we can't do Kiss and Guess at a formal dance,' Ruby says. 'There's a certain protocol. Mommy's friend Shirley Katz has an A-list event planned for us—'

'A, B, C, who cares,' Trish says. 'There aren't any *boys* on the list!'

'OK, girls,' Tina says, 'let's put our thinking caps on.' She motions like she's putting an actual hat on her head. 'What's going to get the boys there? Let's face it, boys hate fancy dances. They're just hoping for some time alone with a pretty . . .'

'I've got an idea,' I say. Tina and Ruby look at me with little hope.

'*Boys*, Willa,' Tina says, '*boys*. How to get a hundred *boys* to the Dream.'

I fluff the curly half of 'the Willa'. 'Trust me', I say, 'I've got a super boy-magnet idea . . . but I've got to make a phone call first.'

'*A super boy-magnet idea*?' Ruby is mimicking my words as I leave.

'Wait a minute, Rube,' Tina says. 'When Willa says "trust me", she delivers.' Tina flips her hair back, done deal.

Now I just have to deliver.

29

Willa's Super Boy-Magnet Idea

We are such stuff as dreams are made on . . .

– Shakespeare, *The Tempest*

Sam is reading the newspaper, shaking his head, when I come down to breakfast. 'That's just not right,' he says.

There's another article on the Bramble Library. Mr Sivler is quoted as saying that, despite community support, the council does not expect the required $35,000 goal to be met in time and that negotiations with the Town of Falmouth are moving along well. 'We believe the residents of Bramble will be even better served by—'

'What!' I am so angry. 'They told Mrs Saperstone twenty-five thousand dollars, not *thirty-five thousand!*'

Stella is just in from her run. 'I knew that Sivler slimeball was up to something,' she says, huffing and sweating. 'I read the article this morning and I was thinking about it on my run. I bet Sivler wants that library property. He's probably got some business venture going. Listen, Willa, we're nearly empty today, just the Kwans and Kauffmans are left. If you want, I'll go with you to lodge a complaint.'

Wow. Stella is taking my side. My throat clenches. 'Thanks, Mother.'

Sam nods at me and winks. 'Go get 'em girls!'

Stella gets dressed for business. I wear my Bramble A uniform. The law offices of Phinneus T. Langerhorn III are three doors down from the Bramble Library. The green ivy hands wave 'good luck' as we pass by.

Mr Langerhorn listens patiently as Stella shrieks and I speak, but in the end, he says he's sorry, there's nothing else he can do. $35,000 by February the fifteenth or else.

This makes my phone call even more urgent.

*

Mama B is delighted to hear from me. She feels horrible about Gramp, but she rallies back when I tell her the news.

'Papa B, come here,' she shouts, dropping the phone. 'We're going back to Bramble. Willa's having another dance.'

I tell Mama B what's going on with the library campaign and how we desperately need the Midwinter Night's Dream to rake in some serious money. And then I tell her my super boy-magnet idea.

'Suzy-Jube will be delighted!' Mama B says. 'She won Miss Daisydew USA and she's on to the Miss American Role Model quarter finals next month. You're getting her right between engagements. Let me put her on.'

Suzy-Jube says 'yes' in a Daisydew minute. 'Insulted? Why of course not, Willa, honey. I'm flattered. If you think I can save your little library, well, consider me booked. Bramble, Cape Cod, here I come! Ya gotta use it or lose it, Mama always says. Use it or lose it. Now . . . what do y'all think I should wear?'

I make up the flyer that night. Suzanna Jubilee's

photo reproduces beautifully. One very lucky Bramble buck is going to win the dream date of his life.

Once the flyers circulate around Bramble Academy, we can't get to the ticket table at lunchtime quick enough to handle the lines of boys. Freshmen, sophomores, juniors, janitors. Tina's old crush, Tanner McGee, is first in line, with the Buoy Boys right behind him. Some guys have been camped out since the lunch ladies cracked the first eggs at dawn. They stare at Suzanna Jubilee's picture and they don't even complain about filling out Tina's compatibly stupid questionnaire.

'It's required,' Tina says.

'Suzanna is going to be there for sure?' the boys ask. 'And the winner gets a date with her for sure?'

'For sure,' Tina says. 'But you have to answer Tina's Ten. No exceptions.'

Tina's Aunt Amber has agreed to input the data and match the couples.

When I asked Tina if I could add a question, she hesitated, but then agreed it would be good to have a 'tie-breaker'. And so we added an eleventh question.

Mrs Sivler takes us in the CJ. 'A little field trip to Boston,' for our gowns.

'The committee is not showing up in otters,' Ruby says.

'Otters,' I say, picturing the animals. 'What do you mean?'

Ruby and Tina roll their eyes.

'OTRs,' Ruby explains. 'Off-the-racks. Absolutely no otters for the planning committee.'

'But, Rube,' Tina says, 'there's really not enough time to do originals . . .'

'Sherry Sivler has ways,' Ruby says. 'Lots and lots of ways. Trust me.'

My gown looks like cotton candy. Pink chiffon with thin rhinestone straps and a heart-shaped neckline. Tina picked a black strapless 'glam'. Ruby will be red – very, very red. When I showed Stella my gown, she got misty-eyed. 'Oh, Willa,' she said. 'Sam, come here! Come look at our girl.'

'I know you think it's all about Cupid,' Tina says to me, 'but aren't you curious if you'll be the most compatible with JFK? He filled out the questionnaire, you know.'

'Don't fudge the results, Tina.'

'I can't,' Tina says. 'The envelopes are sealed. Aunt Amber is the only one who will see the raw data. It will all be computerized and the numbers don't lie.'

'If we're compatibly connected, fine,' I say, 'but I'm not giving up on Cupid.'

Tina laughs. 'How's the flying streaker doing these days anyway?'

'I'm taking a break from taffy,' Nana tells me. She's making a Bramble line of 'conversation hearts', those miniature Valentine's candy hearts with messages stamped on them. 'Sealed with a kiss. Beach bums. Wave Back.' And in the spirit of saving the library: 'You're Booked. Read To Me. Mark My Words. Write On!'

Nana is keeping busy at Sweet Bramble Books. She hired a new assistant and Dr Swammy will be coming on board when Bramble A lets out for the summer.

Bramble is buzzing about Mum and Riley Truth. They're always laughing and holding hands. People are starting to wonder if Riley's planning on moving here.

'Or maybe Mum'll move away with him,' Stella says at dinner one night.

'No,' I say, 'Mum won't leave us.'

Stella and Sam look at each other. 'Well, she looks awfully happy,' Stella says. 'You'd want her to be happy, right?'

30

Swarming Like Locusts

The barge she sat in, like a burnish'd throne,
Burn'd on the water . . .
Purple the sails, and so perfumed, that
The winds were lovesick with them . . .

– Shakespeare, *Antony and Cleopatra*

When the Blazers' limousine pulls up in front of the Bramblebriar Inn, the Buoy Boys just happened to be walking by. Jessie and Luke see Suzy-Jube and stop. They can't move. They can't speak.

That doesn't last for long. Within minutes of Suzanna's arrival, word spreads.

By the time I get back from Mashpee Common, where Tina and Ruby and I were checking on last-minute details for the Dream, boys are swarming like lovesick locusts all over the grounds of

♡ ♡ ♡ 213 ♡ ♡ ♡

the Inn, peaking in windows, climbing trees with binoculars, communicating by walkie-talkie.

There are so many boys, boys, boys, I can barely make my way up the sidewalk. When I finally reach the door, Stella opens it, pulls me in, and locks the door behind us.

'Those boys are *crazy*,' she says. We laugh.

'Where's Suzanna?' I ask.

'Upstairs taking a nap. Chickles says Suzanna needs to rest her vocal chords every afternoon. Her voice needs to be in top shape for her next pageant.'

'What does she sing anyway?' I ask. I never did find out Suzanna's talent.

'Hello, Willa, honey!' Mama B swoops into the room, throwing her arms out for a hug. We hear a voice calling from upstairs. 'Oh good,' Mama B says, 'perfect timing. Here comes my sunshine now.'

We watch as the goddess descends from the heavens. There should be trumpets blaring or the Miss America theme song playing or bluebirds flitting around at least.

'Afternoon, Mama,' Suzanna says. 'Hello, Willa, girl!' She gives me a hug.

'Hi, Suzanna. Thanks so much for coming.'

Sam walks in from the kitchen and takes one good, long look at Suzanna. Stella elbows him. 'We apologize for all the commotion outside,' Stella says.

'Oh, *phish*,' Suzanna says, waving her hand in the air. 'Don't worry about that a'tall. I'm used to it. You just call those sweet boys up on to the porch and I'll make a brief warm-up appearance. Just a howdy-do and see ya at the dance.'

Wait until Tina sees her. Wait until JFK . . . Oh no, what if he wins the date with her? I hadn't even *thought* about that!

Bellford T. comes in and kisses Chickles. 'Is Mama happy?' he asks.

Chickles beams. 'Yes, dear.'

'Good. Cos if Mama ain't happy, nobody ain't happy,' Bellford says, winking at Sam. 'Ain't that right, Sam?'

Ex-English teacher Sam-the-man doesn't even flinch at all the 'ain'ts'. He nods towards Stella. 'That's right, Bellford. We've got to keep these pretty ladies happy.' Stella smiles at him and he winks at her and in that moment it hits me: Stella and Sam are such different people. It would be hard to find ten things they have in common. If they filled out that Perfect Ten compatibility survey I bet Tina's Aunt Amber would have never matched them up. But yet look how much in love they are.

Cupid.

Sam has to call in a Bramble patrol car to escort the boys off the premises. This is so exciting. Tickets for the Dream are sold out. Boys are coming from every high school, from every town on Cape. And wait until JFK sees me in my cotton-candy pink dress. He'll only have eyes for me. Stairway to heaven here we come.

The Midwinter Dream will be perfect. The best dance Bramble has ever seen.

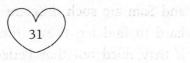

31

Big Spenders

Joy delights in joy.

– Shakespeare, *Sonnet 8*

Early Valentine's Day morning, the morning of the Midwinter Night's Dream, I am bounding down the stairs to help with breakfast when I hear an ear-curdling '*ya-da-yo-ee-yo*'. I turn around quick to look and slip, twisting my foot as I land.

Ouch. I limp to the kitchen for ice. I'll be fine in a minute, just fine.

In an hour the pain is worse. Stella insists we see a doctor.

The film shows a fracture. *No.* They strap on an ugly blue boot.

'Keep that leg elevated tonight,' the cruel, cruel doctor says.

'But the dance is tonight,' I say, first in a somewhat calm voice, and then more hysterically as it becomes clear that Stella will abide by the doctor's orders.

'Willa,' she says, 'I'm so sorry, sweetheart, but we can't be reckless here. The bone needs to heal . . .'

This can't be happening. Shakespeare couldn't have written a more tragic tragedy.

And so here I sit, in my room, all alone, miserable on Valentine's night. Stella and Sam brought me a nice dinner and offered to stay, but it is Valentine's Day, after all, and so I insisted that they keep their date plans. It's bad enough I have to miss the Dream. Who wants to spend Valentine's Day with your parents?

And, in case you haven't figured it out, Suzy-Jube's 'talent' is yodelling.

Seriously. And, believe me, if you heard that labouring-moo-cow sound breaking the sweet silence of morning at the Inn, you'd probably injure yourself somehow too.

Suzanna feels horrible about my accident. So do the Blazers.

They knock on my door before leaving for the dance.

'Come in,' I say, looking out from my pity-party cave of covers.

Suzanna looks like a movie star. No, like a princess. No, like a movie-star princess. Move over Sister Cinderella. Suzy-Jube will be the belle of this ball. I think about my beautiful cotton-candy dress and my sparkly shoes and I fight back the tears.

Mama B's wearing a virtual rainbow of boas . . . red, orange, yellow, green. Papa B is dashing in a white tux with a rainbow top hat, bow tie and cummerbund.

'We were going to surprise you with this at the dance,' Mama B says. She walks toward me, feathers flying. 'Hopefully this will lift your spirits a bit, honey. Go ahead, Papa B, give it to her.'

Papa B hands me an envelope.

It's a thank-you card. Inside there's a picture of what looks like my Bramble Board, except that the mansion behind it is clearly not the Bramble-briar Inn.

'That's our California house,' Papa B explains.

'Read what it says on the Board,' Mama B says.

I hold the picture up closer. 'It is by spending oneself that one becomes rich.'

That was the message I had on the Bramble Board the day the Blazers first visited.

'You don't know how those words changed our lives,' Mama B says. 'Ever since we read your board last October, Willa honey, and ever since you told us about Community Rent at Thanksgiving, we've been spending money left and right.'

'Well, we always spend money left and right,' Papa B says with a laugh, 'but now we're spending it left to build houses for people and right to help kids go to college. And we've never felt so good being such big spenders.'

'That's wonderful,' I say. My eyes fill with tears. I guess Stella was right about the friend-raising. You never know how the good will spread.

'You're a big spender too, Willa,' Mama B says. 'You spend that great big heart of yours.'

Suzanna honks in a tissue and yodels a 'yippee-yay-hoo for Willa'.

'You'd better go or you'll be late,' I say, wiping my nose and laughing.

'Absolutely hootley,' Papa B says. 'Right after you open one more thing. Go ahead, Mama B, give Willa the present.'

It's a cheque made out to the Save the Bramble Library Fund, 'with thanks to our friend Willa Havisham.'

It's enough money to save my library and probably two or three others too.

32

Compatibly Cupid

When you do dance, I wish you
A wave o' the sea, that you might ever do
Nothing but that . . .

— **Shakespeare**, *The Winter's Tale*

I'm imagining the Midwinter Dream in my mind when there's a tap on my window pane. A branch in the wind. Then another tap, louder. Then someone calling my name. I hobble to the window to see.

JFK is standing on the lawn in a tuxedo. I unlatch the window and slide it up.

'Willa,' he shouts. 'Come on down. And bring your coat.'

'I can't.' I laugh. 'I fractured my foot.'

'I've done that before,' JFK says. 'It's in a cast

or something, right? Just go easy on the stairs. I'll meet you at the door.'

I close the window. My heart is pounding. *Breathe, Willa, breathe.*

I look in the mirror. Willa, straight. Willa, curly. I let my curly side rule.

I put on my cotton-candy pink dress and reach for my new cherry lipstick. Right foot, blue boot. Left foot, bunny slipper. So much for the glittery heels.

My heart is racing as I walk down the stairs, slowly, so I won't fall. When I reach the landing I take a deep breath. I wink at the girl in the hallway mirror.

The first thing I notice when I open the door, is that JFK is wearing a red boutonnière. The same colour as Ruby's gown.

'You look pretty,' he says, 'really pretty.' He brushes a curl from my cheek.

The second thing I notice is that there's a light coming from the barn.

'Lean on me,' JFK says, holding out his arm.

I forgot my coat. He gives me his jacket. He leads me towards the barn.

JFK has a flashlight, but the moon is so bright that we don't need it. When I stumble, he picks me up in his arms. 'You're so light,' he says with a laugh.

He's wearing cologne. I'm going to faint. 'Your hair smells good,' he says.

When we reach the barn, he sets me down and opens up the door.

There's a fire glowing in the old silver tub we bobbed for apples in on Halloween. 'Boy Scouts was good for something,' JFK says and laughs.

'How was the dance?' I ask.

'Sort of lame I guess, but your friend Suzanna was a hit.'

'Who won the date with—'

'Here,' JFK says, reaching in his pocket. 'This is for you.'

A little pink box of conversation hearts. There's Cupid on the front.

'Thanks,' I say, disappointed, wishing it was something else.

'It's a belated birthday present,' JFK says. 'Go ahead. Open it.'

There's another box inside the candy. It says Wickstrom's on it.

My hands are shaking. *Oh please let it be*.

Yes. The locket with the tiny gold bow. He must have asked Mr Wickstrom which one I liked. *How sweet*.

'It's beautiful,' I say, my heart pounding like storm waves against the jetty.

I'm afraid to open the heart, but I do.

There are no pictures inside.

I feel sad. I guess I hoped . . . I guess he didn't want to . . .

'The *girl* decides who to put in it,' JFK says, smiling with those gorgeous blue eyes. 'But . . . I hope you decide it's me.'

'Oh, it's you,' I say, hugging him. I'm laughing and crying too.

'It's funny,' JFK says, 'but guess who my match was for that compatible couple thing?

Me, I'm hoping, *me*. 'I don't know, who?'

'You.'

'Really?' So Tina was right after all.

'Well, actually,' JFK says, 'it was you and another girl too.'

What other girl?

'But the eleventh question broke the tie,' JFK says. 'Do you remember what you wrote?'

'Of course. I said I have so many favourite books, that I couldn't pick just one.'

JFK laughs. 'Well I guess we've got that in common and at least ten other things too. Oh, and Tina said to tell you she "told you so" – and that you and I are "compatibly perfect".'

'Make that *compatibly cupid*,' I say.

'*What* . . .' JFK starts to ask, but before he can finish, I kiss him.

'You taste like cherries,' he says with a laugh.

'You taste like peppermint.'

He fastens the locket around my neck. 'Now, how about a dance?'

And so we dance, in gown and tuxedo, on this midwinter night in the barn. And it isn't a dream and I'm certain I hear 'Stairway to Heaven' playing.

And as we dance, careful of my foot, the fire crackling warm beside us, I see something flitter up in the rafters. *Nice work, baby, nice work.*

THE END
(or, as Will would say . . . 'All's well that ends well.' ☺)

Willa's Pix 2

(see *The Wedding Planner's Daughter* for the original Willa's Pix)

Bird by Bird Anne Lamott
A Christmas Memory Truman Capote
The Complete Works of Shakespeare
A Day No Pigs Would Die Robert Newton Peck
The Education of Little Tree Forrest Carter
Fahrenheit 451 Ray Bradbury
The Giver Lois Lowry
The Great Gilly Hopkins Katherine Paterson
Moby Dick Herman Melville
The Outsiders S. E. Hinton
Pollyanna Eleanor H. Porter
Roll of Thunder, Hear My Cry Mildred D. Taylor
A Tale of Two Cities Charles Dickens
Treasure Island Robert Louis Stevenson
A Tree Grows in Brooklyn Betty Smith
The Witch of Blackbird Pond Elizabeth George Speare

Acknowledgements

With sincerest thanks to:

My beautiful sister, Noreen Mahoney, the biggest heart in Brewster, and to Mike, Ryan and Jack Mahoney; my editor, Alyssa Eisner, Willa's true fairy godmother; my agent, Tracey Adams, and to Josh and Abby Adams and Karen Riskin; my brother, Jerry Murtagh, for his inspirational love; my son Christopher, who said 'it's like poetry, but it's music'; my goddaughter, Lauren Murtagh, for the 'wishing fountain' and to Kevin, Col, Liam and Brendan; to Sheila Murphy for 'Community Rent'; Lenny and Barb Noel for the 'honey-do list'; Kim McMann of the Troy Public Library for reminding me how we 'signed-out' books; Leslie Saperstone of the Guilderland Public Library for years of encouragement; and to all librarians, booksellers and teachers who match us with books; to my wonderful critique buddies Debbi Michiko Florence, Kyra Teis, Nancy Castaldo, Ellen Laird, Karen Beil, Rose Kent, Liza Frenette, Lois Feister Huey, Jackie Rogers and especially

Acknowledgements

Jennifer Groff, luminous librarian, writer and friend; to my dancing buddies Kathy Johnson, Ellen Donovan and Paula Davenport; and to my amazingly supportive and loving family: my sons, Chris, Connor and Dylan, and my husband, Tony Paratore. *You are my greatest joys.*

C.M.P., 2006

A selected list of titles available from Macmillan Children's Books

The prices shown below are correct at the time of going to press. However, Macmillan Publishers reserves the right to show new retail prices on covers, which may differ from those previously advertised.

All Pan Macmillan titles can be ordered from our website, www.panmacmillan.com, or from your local bookshop and are also available by post from:

Bookpost, PO Box 29, Douglas, Isle of Man IM99 1BQ
Credit cards accepted. For details:
Telephone: 01624 677237
Fax: 01624 670923
Email: bookshop@enterprise.net
www.bookpost.co.uk

Free postage and packing in the United Kingdom